Dear Reader,

Looking back over the years, I find it hard to realize that twenty-six of them have gone by since I wrote my first book—*Sister Peters in Amsterdam*. It wasn't until I started writing about her that I found that once I had started writing, nothing was going to make me stop—and at that time I had no intention of sending the manuscript to a publisher. It was my daughter who urged me to try my luck.

I shall never forget the thrill of having my first book accepted. And it's still a thrill each time a new story is accepted. Writing is such a pleasure to me, and seeing a story unfolding on my old typewriter is like watching a film and wondering how it will end. Happily, of course.

To have so many of my books republished is such a delightful thing to happen, and I can only hope that those who read them will share my pleasure in seeing them on the bookshelves again...and will enjoy reading them.

Betty Neels

Betty Neels spent her childhood and youth in Devonshire before training as a nurse and midwife. She was an army nursing sister during the war, married a Dutchman and subsequently lived in Holland for fourteen years. She now lives with her husband in Dorset and has a daughter and grandson. Her hobbies are reading, animals, old buildings and, of course, writing. Betty started to write upon retirement from nursing, incited by a lady in a library bemoaning the lack of romantic novels. She has since become one of Harlequin's most prolific and well-loved authors.

THE BEST of
BETTY NEELS

MAGIC IN VIENNA

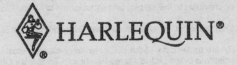

HARLEQUIN®

TORONTO • NEW YORK • LONDON
AMSTERDAM • PARIS • SYDNEY • HAMBURG
STOCKHOLM • ATHENS • TOKYO • MILAN • MADRID
PRAGUE • WARSAW • BUDAPEST • AUCKLAND

ISBN 0-373-51130-2

MAGIC IN VIENNA

First North American Publication 2001

Copyright © 1985 by Betty Neels.

This edition published by arrangement with Harlequin Books S.A.

® and TM are trademarks of the publisher. Trademarks indicated with ® are registered in the United States Patent and Trademark Office, the Canadian Trade Marks Office and in other countries.

Visit us at www.eHarlequin.com

Printed in U.S.A.

CHAPTER ONE

THE ROOM WAS large, shabbily furnished and inadequately heated by old fashioned radiators, its discomforts heightened by virtue of the dull April morning. Its occupants sat round the heavy old fashioned table in the middle of the room eating their breakfast, presided over by a young woman whose large, long lashed hazel eyes redeemed an otherwise ordinary face from plainness. She was very neat, with pale brown hair coiled on the top of her head. As much of her person as was visible above the table, was clad in a knitted sweater which looked faded by most standards but was carefully pressed. She poured tea from the large pot before her while she listened to a girl of fifteen or so, sitting at the other end of the table. The girl was pretty, fair haired and blue eyed, her prettiness marred by a sulky mouth.

'I think Mother's mean to make me have my meals with you and the children,' she declared. 'Just because she swans around with her boyfriends and doesn't want any competition I have to stay here in the schoolroom. Well, I won't and no one can stop me.'

She glared defiantly at the girl she was addressing who said bracingly, 'Don't talk like that in front of the children, Chloë. Why don't you go down presently and have a talk with your mother? But you are only fifteen you know.'

The boy sitting between them spoke with a full mouth. 'Much good that'll do you.' He thrust his cup down the table. 'Give me some more tea, Cordelia.'

'Please...'

He turned pale blue eyes on her. 'Why should I say please? Mother treats you like a servant so I shall too.'

The hazel eyes took fire but her voice was steady and quiet. 'We shared the same father, Matthew.'

'And he's dead. You'll be stuck here with the twins for years because you've nowhere to go.'

The girl didn't bother to answer but turned her attention to the two small children sitting at the other side of the table. Six year old twins, a boy and a girl, eating bread and butter and jam and taking no notice of anyone. She had done her best to love them but they weren't lovable children; her father had died soon after they were born and since her stepmother, who had never wanted them in the first place, ignored them as much as possible, she had tried to be a mother to them, more for her father's sake, she supposed, for she had loved him. But now after six years, she had to admit that she had very little affection for them, largely because they had shown her none. She remembered very clearly her shock and apprehension when her father had told her that he was to marry again, and produced, almost immediately, a stepmother with two children of her own from a former marriage. Chloë and Matthew had been quite small then but they had looked at her with hostile eyes and although she had done her best to get on good terms with them, she had been defeated, largely because her stepmother had encouraged them, almost from the first day, to treat her as a kind of superior servant. It had been done very subtly, so that her father never had an inkling of what was going on and her stepmother had always been careful to behave charmingly towards her when her father was with them. Cordelia, a girl of spirit but sensible as well, could see no good coming of bringing the true state of affairs to his notice, and now all these years later, she was glad that she hadn't.

But now the children didn't need her; true, they expected her to look after them, much as a governess would, but even the twins at school each day, were quite able to look after themselves. Matthew had just remarked gloatingly that there was nowhere for her to go, but she had every intention of leaving. For several weeks now she had scanned the jobs columns in the newspapers and although there had been nothing which she felt she could tackle, she went on looking. Sooner or later, someone would want a young woman willing and able to cope with a child or children. True, it might mean going from the frying pan into the fire, but at least she would be paid. At present, she had no money of her own; from time to time her stepmother would give her cash for shoes or clothes, but she was expected to make it last and whatever she bought was expected to last, too.

Chloë pushed back her chair and got up from the table. 'I'm going to see Mother now,' she declared.

'Your mother doesn't like to be disturbed while

she's having her breakfast,' Cordelia pointed out. 'I should wait if I were you.'

'Well, I'm not you,' said Chloë rudely, 'and I'll do what I like.'

Matthew got up too. 'I'm going fishing,' he threw over his shoulder. It was nearly the end of the Easter holiday, and Cordelia sighed with relief because in another couple of days he'd be back at school. She finished the tea in her cup and remembered that the twins had been invited to a friend's house for the morning. She didn't like the boy they were to visit; he was almost, but not quite a vandal although he was barely eight years old, but her stepmother was a friend of his mother's and would hear no word against him. They would be unmanageable when they got back from there for lunch, but at least it would leave the morning free for her to get on with sorting out Matthew's school uniform. She stood over them while they washed their hands and tidied themselves, saw them safely down the short drive and across the village green and then walked briskly back to the house, a red brick Edwardian residence, over embellished with fancy brick work and balconies. Cordelia had never liked it; they had moved there just before her father had died because her stepmother had complained that the little Regency house in a nearby village was far too small. Her father had been ill then, too ill to stand firm against his wife's insistence, and he'd given in without argument. If I manage to get a job, thought Cordelia, I shan't miss home at all, for it isn't a home.

The papers were in the hall as she went in. The

cook and daily maid were in the kitchen, her step-mother wouldn't come downstairs for another hour. Cordelia snatched up the *Telegraph* and the *Times* and sat herself down to read the jobs columns. There weren't many in the household sections, the only ones she felt fitted for. She scanned first one paper and then the second one. Almost at the end of the column her eye lighted on what could only be an answer to her prayers. A patient, good tempered young woman, well-educated and with experience in the management of children was required to accompany a lady and her young granddaughter to Vienna where she would hand over her charge to her uncle. The post was temporary and references were required.

Cordelia flew upstairs to the second floor where she had a room. It was as shabby as the schoolroom and whereas the other rooms in the house were all hand-somely furnished, it hadn't been considered necessary to offer her one of them. All the same, it was hers, and had her few small treasures and a little desk of her mother's there. She sat down at it and wrote a reply, stating that she was twenty-six, had six years of experience with children, had been educated at a well known girl's school and offered the family doc-tor's name together with that of her father's solicitor as reference. She would have to post the letter at once as well as telephone these two gentlemen but first of all she would have to return the papers to the table in the hall. She had barely arranged them neatly and was turning away to go upstairs again when her step-mother came down.

She nodded at Cordelia's polite good morning,

picked up the papers and crossed the hall to the sitting room.

'I'll be out this morning, you will all have lunch in the schoolroom and I wish you'd press that skirt of mine—that maid's no good. And you can go down to the village and get the groceries for cook, she says she must have them here this morning.' She turned and looked at Cordelia with a cold eye: 'And you can stop putting silly ideas into Chloë's head—I won't have her downstairs when I have guests. Her manners are appalling, surely to goodness you can at least teach the children how to behave? You've little else to do.'

Cordelia said quietly, 'The twins to look after, Matthew to try to discipline, their clothes to see to, the shopping, the ironing quite often, the...'

Her stepmother lifted a hand. 'You ungrateful girl, whining at me in such a fashion. You have a home and food and...' she paused.

'And what?' asked Cordelia gently. Mrs Gibson glared, went into the sitting room and shut the door with a snap.

There was no sign of Chloë and Cordelia didn't want to see her for a bit. She nipped smartly upstairs, found her purse, woefully slim, put the letter in her skirt pocket and hurried out of the house. There was a telephone kiosk near the general stores and post office, she 'phoned the doctor first, extracted a promise that he would write a glowing reference for her if it was asked for, and then got on to the solicitor, an old man now, who had been a great friend of her father's and was easily persuaded to do as she asked and not say a word to anyone. Both gentlemen were aware that her life hadn't been an easy one since her father's death and she was, after all, not a young silly girl. She bought her groceries and went back with her loaded basket to spend the rest of the morning listening to Chloë's furious invective, mostly and quite unfairly directed against herself.

She had taken the precaution of asking the advertiser not to telephone and it was two days before the letter came. The postman came early but Cordelia was already up, helping Cook with the breakfast and laying the table. Cook, who had been with the family for a matter of twenty years, had strong feelings about the way in which Cordelia was put upon. 'The master would turn in his grave if he did but know,' she observed indignantly to her croney, the rectory housekeeper, 'but Miss Cordelia, bless her, just goes sailing on, won't be browbeaten, mind you, but never complains nor says a word to anyone. It fair breaks your heart. It's to be hoped that something will happen.'

The letter happened. Cordelia was invited to call at Brown's Hotel in London on the following Saturday at two o'clock for an interview. She read the letter twice and then put it in her pocket and Cook, who had been standing on the other side of the kitchen stove, watching her read it, asked, 'Good news, Miss Cordelia?'

Cordelia explained. 'And don't please say a word to anyone,' she begged, 'but how on earth am I to get there?'

Cook couldn't help her; Cordelia spent the morning plotting ways and means and didn't come up with a single feasible idea, but someone was on her side; call it Fate, her Fairy Godmother, or just plain Luck, that afternoon her stepmother told her that she would be away for the weekend. 'Friends in Berkshire,' she said languidly, 'I'll drive myself and I'll have to take Chloë with me, I suppose, they want to see her— Godparents, you know. The twins are to spend the day with the Kings; you'd better take them over directly after breakfast and fetch them back by seven o'clock. Matthew's back at school, isn't he?'

'He goes tomorrow.'

'So you'll have nothing to do on Saturday—you'd better turn out the schoolroom. And see that Chloë's things are ready by Friday afternoon; I want to leave after lunch.'

There were three days to go; Cordelia wrote a polite note confirming her interview, counted her money and worked out bus times to fit in with trains from St Albans. The buses didn't fit in; she would never be able to catch the morning bus from the village although she thought she would be able to catch the early evening bus back from St Albans; there was one at five o'clock too, she might manage to catch that one. A taxi was the answer but she hadn't enough money. She went through her usual chores worrying away at her problems and by Friday morning she still hadn't solved it. She had gone to the kitchen to fetch the tray for breakfast when Cook stopped her. 'Something's on your mind, Miss Cordelia?'

'Well, I don't think I'll be able to get to London— there's no bus to get me to St Albans. I'll have to 'phone and cancel the whole thing.'

Cook turned the bacon she was frying. 'No need, dearie, my nephew Sam he's going to London tomorrow—he'll take you the whole way and be glad to do it.'

Cordelia put down her tray. 'Cook, you angel. Will he really? I'll pay my share of the petrol...'

'Indeed you won't, Miss Cordelia, for it's not costing him anything extra and he'll have company. He won't be able to bring you back though...'

'That's okay—there are several trains in the late afternoon and the last bus for the village doesn't leave St Albans until six-fifteen, though I'll try and catch the one before that if I can.' Distant shouts signalled the twins clattering along to the schoolroom, and she picked up her tray once more. 'What time?' she asked. 'I'm to be there by two o'clock.'

'Sam wants to be at his aunt's by one o'clock. If I do you some sandwiches will you be able to eat them somewhere?'

'Bless you Cook, of course, I will.'

'Well, good luck, Miss Cordelia, you deserve a taste of the world. I'll miss you.'

'I shall miss you too, if I get the job.'

Nothing occurred to upset their plans, her stepmother and Chloë left after lunch and since it was a fine afternoon, Cordelia took the twins for a walk, gave them their tea and then played cards with them until bedtime. They didn't want to go, of course, but the reminder that they were to spend the day with Johnny and Jennifer and would have to get up smartly in the morning, got them into bed at last. Cordelia ate her supper in the schoolroom and repaired to her own room to prepare for the next day. She had had her suit for quite a time now, it was well cut and fitted her nicely and though it was sadly out of fashion it would have to do. She polished her shoes put handbag and gloves ready and went to bed. She went to sleep at once; there was no point in lying awake worrying about the interview, she had learnt long ago not to worry too much but to make the best of what was offered.

She enjoyed the ride with Sam; the twins safely seen into the Kings' household she had been free to get dressed, drink a hasty cup of coffee, and with Cook's promise to see that the schoolroom cupboard was turned out and the furniture polished, she had got into his small, down-at-heel van with something like excitement. Only when he drew up in front of the dignified exterior of Brown's Hotel did she falter.

'Looks a bit grand,' ventured Sam, peering at the windowboxes.

Cordelia, with memories of visiting such hotels in her father's company before he remarried, was made of sterner stuff. 'It's only an hotel,' she pointed out. 'And I shall just go to a room to be interviewed. Thank you, Sam, for the lift. You've no idea how grateful I am.' She beamed at him. 'Perhaps, one day I'll be able to repay it.' She got out of the van and ignoring the surprise on the face of the doorman, put her head through the open window. 'Have a nice weekend with your auntie.'

She crossed the pavement. 'I've an appointment with Lady Trescombe,' she told the doorman, 'Where should I go?'

The doorman was elderly and had elderly ideas. Now here's a lady, he told himself, not like some of those flighty young things I've been opening the door to. Aloud he said politely; 'If you go to the desk, the clerk will help you.' He held the door for her and she thanked him as he escorted her inside.

Lady Trescombe had a room on the first floor and she was shown into a small ante room leading to it. To her bitter surprise there were three other girls already there. They eyed her, dismissed her as not worth worrying about, and ignored her 'Good afternoon' as she sat down.

They were all smartly dressed, a good deal younger than she was, moreover they each one of them wore the look of someone who had enjoyed a good meal. The sandwiches which she and Sam had shared in a lay-by hadn't really filled her and she longed for a cup of tea. Worse still, she was far too early; there was the best part of an hour before her appointment. A girl came out, looking pleased with herself and one of the others got up and went through the door into the room beyond. Cordelia, realising that she had a long wait before her, allowed her thoughts to dwell on the unlikely possibility of her getting the job and if she did what she would do with the money she earned, and more important, what she would do when the job finished. How long was temporary, she wondered, a week, a month, six months? And once embarked on a life of her own, should she stick to similar work or should she find work in a shop or train as a nurse or even become someone's housekeeper? One thing was certain, she would never go back to her stepmother's house.

She sat on patiently as the other girls, one by one, went away and returned until at last she was the only one left, and presently the girl before her came out, said, 'You next,' and left too.

Cordelia took a deep breath and opened the door. The room was large, comfortably furnished and warm. She hadn't formed any idea of the person whom she was to meet and the rather fragile elderly lady sitting in an easy chair by a small table, took her by surprise. She said good afternoon in her pleasant voice and at a nod, sat down on a chair drawn up close to the table.

The lady might look fragile but she also looked very alert and a little severe. She had a small voice but the questions she put were very much to the point. No, said Cordelia, she had no university degree, and no, she hadn't worked for anyone before, and no, she couldn't drive a car. It made a nice change when she was able to say that yes she could speak German after a fashion, that she had spent quite a few years looking after the young stepbrothers and sisters, that she had no plans to marry and no romantic attachment, as Lady Trescombe put it.

'Why do you want this job?' asked that woman suddenly.

'I've been looking after the children since my father remarried,' explained Cordelia, 'the twins are six years old and go to school. I'm not really needed at home.'

'You won't be missed?'

'No.'

'My granddaughter,' said Lady Trescombe, 'is a spoilt child but a nice one, she is twelve years old and her parents have been in South America for two years. She has been living with me but my son has decided that I should have a rest and has agreed to have Eileen to live with him until his sister and her husband return home in a few months' time. I believe that you will suit very well, but I must warn you that your stay in Vienna will depend on whether he wishes you to remain as Eileen's companion. She will, of course, be sent to school but you will be kept fully occupied. My son is a surgeon, working at a hospital there. He expects to return to England sometime this summer.' She paused and mentioned a salary which sent Cordelia's blood pressure sky high. 'Do you wish to consider my offer or are you prepared to accept it at once.'

'I'll accept it, thank you. I think I should tell you though that my stepmother will probably be annoyed because I want to earn my own living...'

'No doubt,' agreed Lady Trescombe drily, 'If it will help at all, I will write to her.'

Cordelia hesitated. 'Well, that would be marvellous, but I don't want to—to hide behind you, Lady Trescombe.'

'I fancy that you are not in the habit of hiding behind anyone, Miss Gibson. Let me see, it is now the last week of April, I wish to travel in one month's time. I should be obliged if you will take up your post two weeks before that so that Eileen may get to know you. That will make it around the twenty-third of the month. Will you arrange that? I think it may be best if I send the car for you.'

She smiled suddenly. 'I believe that we shall understand each other very well. Will you have a cup of tea before you go? I intend to have one, interviewing is dry work. If you would be so good as to 'phone down? Tea and buttered toast.'

Cordelia with rumbling insides, thankfully accepted and did as she was bidden, and when tea came, ate the delicious, thin slivers of buttery toast with slow daintiness, subduing an urge to bolt the lot.

Lady Trescombe, it transpired, lived just outside Guildford and it was there that Cordelia would go to start with. 'You will naturally have time to do whatever shopping you may need,' she pointed out and eyed Cordelia's unassuming appearance. She added, probably due to her scrutiny, 'I daresay that you have very little need for town clothes since you live in the country; I suggest that I advance you a part of your salary so that you may buy anything you might need, but we can discuss that later.' She put down her cup and saucer and said with a smile: 'I think that is all, unless you have any questions?'

'Not at the moment, thank you, Lady Trescombe.' Cordelia had got up, sensing that the interview was over. 'I shall do my best with Eileen and I'm most grateful for being given the chance to work for you.'

They shook hands and Lady Trescombe said: 'I'll write and confirm this and also write, as I suggested, to your stepmother. I must warn you again, though, that if my son doesn't wish to have you remain with

Eileen in Vienna the job may only last a fortnight or so.'

'I understand that,' Cordelia's voice was quite firm; she had her chance and she was going to seize it with both hands and not worry too much about what would happen next. She thought that she had a good chance of staying; middle aged bachelors might not take too kindly to someone young and pretty invading their calm households, but she was neither, she had learnt long ago to merge into the background and she would go on doing that if necessary.

The doorman touched his cap as she left the hotel and offered to get her a taxi. She beamed at him, suddenly delighted with her world. 'I'll walk, thank you,' she told him and set off briskly and turned the corner in to Grafton Street and thence as fast as she could go into Regent Street. If she didn't have to wait too long for a bus she would be able to catch the five o'clock train.

She got back in good time to fetch the twins, who had, she gathered from Mrs King's veiled remarks, behaved badly. They were both peevish and almost unmanageable; getting them to bed took all her patience and most of her strength. Lady Trescombe had warned her that her granddaughter was spoilt but at least there was only one of her, thought Cordelia, as she ate her supper later on. She was sharing it with Cook, pouring into that sympathetic lady's ears all the excitements of her day.

'It sounds a treat,' commented Cook, 'and depend upon it, you being such a nice young lady, the gentleman will want you to stay, Miss Cordelia.'

Cordelia hoped most fervently that that would be so. The letter offering her the job, arrived on Monday, so did a letter for her stepmother who read it with outraged disapproval and then subjected Cordelia to half an hour's invective and reproaches. Not that they made any difference to Cordelia, who listened with a calm patience which served to annoy that lady even more.

But beyond railing at her, there was very little her stepmother could do; she was a grown woman, penniless it was true, but independent. She suggested quietly that her stepmother should advertise for an *au pair* or a home help to take her place and then went up to the attics to search for the suit case she had used years ago when she had gone to boarding school. It was shabby, but it would have to do. She carried it down to her room and cleaned it up and put it in the bottom of the old fashioned wardrobe; it gave her a nice feeling of security although there were three weeks before she could take up her new job.

Chloë and the twins took the news that she was leaving with little interest although they grumbled a good deal at the idea of having someone in her place. Not because they minded her going, Chloë was quick to point out, but because their mother had warned them that whoever came would be able to go again whenever she liked, unlike their ungrateful stepsister, she had added nastily. And since she had no intention of engaging a series of *au pairs*, they would have to behave themselves. 'But of course,' said Chloë rudely, 'I'll do exactly what I like; I've never listened to you, and I don't intend to listen to whoever comes, whatever Mother says.'

Cordelia hadn't answered; they were all making life as hard as possible for the last week or two, but she hardly noticed; she thought a great deal about the girl she was to look after and speculated a good deal about the uncle in Vienna. Lady Trescombe was in her sixties, she guessed, which meant that her son would probably be verging on forty or perhaps older than that; a balding misogynist probably, since he wasn't married, quite likely he didn't much like children, and she and Eileen would have to keep out of his way. Of course, mused Cordelia, he might take an interest, but he also might take an instant dislike to herself and send her packing, but at least he would have to pay her fare back and she would have a little money. She refused to think beyond that; she had waited a long while for something to happen and now that it had, she refused to believe that anything could go wrong.

The three weeks went very slowly but she went around the house doing the chores she had always done and whenever she could, went to her room and did what she could with her meagre wardrobe. She looked with dislike at each garment in turn, really there was nothing fit to wear except a handful of woollies and a sober mouse-coloured dress. She would have to spend all the money she was to have advanced; fortunately it was almost summer and she could get by with a skirt and blouses and perhaps a jacket; there was the question of something decent to wear in the evening too—a long skirt and a couple of blouses might do. If only she could lay her hands on a sewing machine and some material... She might have borrowed the former from someone in the village but she had no more than a pound or two in her purse and very little opportunity to go to St Albans. She would have to do the best she could once she got to Guildford and in the meantime she washed and ironed and pressed and thought happily of the new clothes she would buy.

Her stepmother hardly spoke to her and when, at last the day of her departure arrived, a splendidly warm sunny morning too, so that Cordelia felt all wrong in the grey dress, Mrs Gibson turned her back on her when her stepdaughter went along to her room to say goodbye.

'Don't think you can come back here, Cordelia, I'm sure I don't want to see you again—the ingratitude...'

Cordelia went out of the room without a word; Chloë was in the schoolroom reading; she glanced up for a moment as Cordelia went in, said goodbye carelessly and went back to her reading. The twins had already gone to school with never a backward glance. She went to the kitchen and took her leave of Cook, who began to cry. 'There are those who'll be sorry for this,' she uttered fiercely, 'letting you go without so much as a pound note and wearing clothes I wouldn't give to the jumble! begging your pardon, Miss Cordelia.' She pressed a small packet into Cordelia's hand. 'Don't open it now, love—it's just a little something so that you will remember me. And the village wishes you well, you know that. Write when you have time...'

'Of course I shall, Cook, and thank you for your present.' Cordelia bent and kissed the elderly cheek. 'I'm sure I'm going to be happy.' And since Cook was still weeping she added cheerfully: 'I'll meet a rich man who'll fall head over heels in love with me and we'll set up house and you shall come and cook for us.'

Cook blew her nose and wiped her eyes. 'You mean that, Miss Cordelia? Then don't leave it too long, will you? I've been thinking of leaving these last few months, but I'm getting on a bit and there aren't many jobs going...'

Cordelia took her hands in hers. 'That's a promise, Cook. Now I must go.'

She carried her case down to the front door after breakfast, Lady Trescombe had said the car would be there at half-past nine and it was exactly that time. She picked up her case and went outside and the elderly man sitting behind the wheel of a Daimler motor car, got out and took it from her with a cheerful: 'Good morning, Miss. I'm Bates, the chauffeur.' He cast an eye over her neat, unspectacular person and smiled very kindly at her. 'Welcome to Lady Trescombe's household.' He held the door of the car open but Cordelia hesitated: 'May I sit in front with you, Bates? You see, I don't know much about anything. I don't mean to pry, but it would be a great help if you could tell me a little about Lady Trescombe and her granddaughter—it's the first time I've had a job you see, and I'm not sure about things...'

Bates shut the car door and ushered her into the seat beside his. 'Well, now, Miss, where shall I start?'

He started the car and drove smoothly away and Cordelia didn't look back.

By the time they were nearing Guildford she knew quite a lot; Lady Trescombe was the finest lady anyone could work for; not strong but always kind and good tempered. As for the staff, there was himself, his wife who cooked for them all, Elsie the parlour maid who also looked after Lady Trescombe, and Mrs Trump and Miss Gage who came in daily. 'And then there's you Miss and our Miss Eileen. A very nice little girl—a bit lively as you might say, but she being the only one is used to having her own way. You like children, Miss?'

'Yes, Bates, I do.' She thought briefly of the twins whom she would so gladly have loved if only they had let her. 'I hope we shall get on well together.'

They were on the outskirts of Guildford now, bypassing the town and going beyond it into the countryside once more. They were almost on the edge of a small village when Bates swinging the car between brick gate posts went, more slowly now, up a short drive to a pleasant red brick house, old and beautifully maintained, it's latticed windows shining in the sunshine.

Cordelia had been sternly suppressing panic for the last few miles and all for nothing; nothing could have been kinder than her reception as she went through the door held open by Bates.

It was Mrs Bates, short, stout and cheerful, who trotted into the hall, closely followed by Lady Trescombe and in the little flurry of greetings and instructions about her luggage and the urging into the sitting room where coffee was waiting, she forgot her panic. Presently, when she had drunk her coffee while Lady Trescombe chatted about nothing in particular, she was taken up the oak staircase to a room at the back of the house so that she might unpack and settle in, as Mrs Bates cosily put it.

Alone, Cordelia sat down on the edge of the bed and looked around her. The room was square, neither too big nor too small, with a wide latticed window and a low beamed ceiling. It was furnished simply but with great comfort with well polished oak and flowery chintz. There was a thick quilt on the bed and a small easy chair upholstered in pink velvet by the fireplace as well as a writing desk under the window and flowers and books on the bedside table. She took it all in slowly; after the bare austerity of her own bedroom this was heaven indeed. She went over to the cupboard along one wall and peered into its roomy interior; her clothes would be swallowed up in it. There was a bathroom too, pale pink, with thick fluffy towels and a shelf filled with soaps and bath salts. Cordelia shut her eyes and then opened them again, just to make sure that she wasn't dreaming.

It was real enough; she gave a long happy sigh and unpacked.

When she went downstairs again she found Lady Trescombe sitting in the drawing room where they had had coffee. She would have to ask just what her duties were and what better than to do it at once? Only she wasn't given the chance. Lady Trescombe put down the book she was reading and smiled at her.

'I thought it might be best for you to go into the

garden and meet Eileen on your own. She will be at the very end, behind the beech hedge I expect. She knows that you will be accompanying us to Vienna but I didn't tell her you would be coming today. And may I call you Cordelia?'

'Of course, Lady Trescombe, and I'd like Eileen to call me that too, if you don't mind.'

'I think it a very good idea. Get to know each other today and tomorrow we'll work out some kind of routine. You will want to go shopping—perhaps in two or three days time? Did I tell you how we are travelling?'

Cordelia shook her head. 'No, Lady Trescombe.'

'We fly to Munich and take a small cruise ship down the Danube. A slow way to get to Vienna perhaps, but we shall have a week to get to know each other and if Eileen is feeling doubtful about meeting her uncle and her life with him, you will have the opportunity to reassure her. I should warn you that I intend to do nothing during the week; I shall rely upon you to entertain Eileen and keep her happy; we shall meet for lunch and dinner of course, but I shall put you in sole charge.'

She gave Cordelia a questioning look as she spoke and Cordelia returned the look calmly; if Lady Trescombe was hinting delicately that Eileen was going to be difficult she refused to let it fluster her; no one, she considered, could be more difficult than her own stepsister; if she could emerge unscathed from a number of years of dealing with tantrums and rudeness and not be paid for it either, then she could certainly cope with Eileen. She stood up. 'I'll go and meet her now, shall I?'

The french windows were open on to the garden beyond and she strolled off, making for the beech hedge in as casual a manner as she could manage. She had no doubt that Lady Trescombe would be watching from the house to see if she were showing any signs of nerves. She reached the beech hedge and went, still unhurriedly, beyond it and, just as Lady Trescombe had said, found Eileen lying on the grass reading.

She hadn't heard Cordelia, so there was time to study her; she was tall for her age, Cordelia judged, and slim to the point of thinness. She had an untidy mane of dark curly hair and denim trousers and a cotton top which she wore, although crumpled, were exactly what a clothes conscious child of her age would choose.

Cordelia couldn't see her face; she stepped heavily and deliberately on to the paved path between the hedge and the child looked up. She had been crying, evident from puffed eyelids and a pink nose, neither of which could disguise a pretty face. But the scowl on it wasn't pretty as she jumped to her feet.

'Who are you?' she demanded, and then: 'You're the governess Granny said she'd found. Well, I'm not going to like you for a start...'

Cordelia didn't smile. She said coolly. 'I've lived most of my life with two stepsisters and two step-brothers and none of them liked me. I'm a bit disappointed that you won't even give me a trial, but I admire your honesty. Only I think you at least owe me an explanation as to why you're crying. Because of me?'

'No, of course not. I didn't know what you'd be like, did I?'

'That's something. Do you want to tell me?'

Eileen stared at her. 'You're not a bit what I thought you'd be.'

Cordelia made herself comfortable on a tree stump. 'What did you expect?'

'Well—someone old and plain and cross.'

'I'm plain but I'm not that old and I don't think I'm often cross, suppose you give me a trial?'

Eileen looked surprised. 'Well—all right. Do you really want to know why I was crying?' She added fiercely. 'I don't cry much.'

'Yes, I'd like to know. I'm not curious, mind you—but perhaps, seeing that I'm a complete stranger, I might be able to help a bit.'

'It's going away from here and Granny. Mummy and Daddy won't be coming home for two months and now Uncle Charles says she must have a rest from looking after me and so I have to go and live with him in Vienna until they come home. There's no one else you see.'

'You don't like your Uncle?'

'I don't remember him. He's a surgeon and he's always busy, I was a little girl when I saw him last, but I can't remember him very well. He's very large and quite old. I'll have to be quiet in his house and I don't suppose he'll want to see me much…'

'He sounds a bit dreary,' agreed Cordelia, conjuring up a picture of a learned, slightly stooping gen-

tleman, going bald, probably with a drooping mous-
tache and a dislike of children, 'but as long as we
keep out of his way and don't annoy him, I should
think we'd quite enjoy ourselves. I've never been to
Vienna but I believe it's an exciting sort of place.
Two months isn't long, you know, and I daresay we'll
be able to fill in the days until your mother and father
come home.' Always supposing, she told herself silently, that uncle didn't dislike her on sight and send
her back to England.

Eileen gave her a childish grin. 'I think perhaps I'll
like you,' she observed. 'Why didn't your stepsisters
and brothers like you?'

Cordelia pondered the question. 'Well, my father
married again, a widow with a little girl and boy, and
they didn't like me overmuch, I suppose because I
was grown up and they weren't, and then my stepmother had twins, and I looked after them. I expect
they thought of me as a kind of nursemaid.'

'You're not sorry for yourself?' stated Eileen.

'Good grief no. I say Eileen, I have to buy some
clothes before we go to Vienna, would you help me
with that? You see, I've been living in the country
and I'm not a bit fashionable.'

'I can see that. What's your name?'

'Cordelia.'

Eileen smiled, a wide friendly smile, Cordelia was
relieved to see. 'OK Cordelia, I think you're nice.'

'Thank you Eileen, I think you're nice too. You
must tell me what I'm supposed to do, you know. Do
you think we ought to go and find your grandmother
and tell her that we've met?'

Eileen came closer and took her hand. 'Yes, let's.'

CHAPTER TWO

IT WAS GOING to be all right, decided Cordelia, lying
awake in her comfortable bed that first night; the day
had gone well. She and Eileen had lunched with Lady
Trescombe and then gone for a leisurely walk while
the child advised her solemnly about the kind of
clothes she should buy and the various improvements
she could make to her hair and make-up. Then when
that important subject had been dealt with, they made
hilarious guesses about Uncle Charles; he was to be
stout and short, going bald and stuffy and when Cordelia reminded Eileen that she had said that he was a
large man, she was told that people shrank with age.
But they didn't talk about him at tea, after all Lady
Trescombe was his mother, and might be sensitive
about his appearance. 'And in any case,' observed
Cordelia, going to say good night, 'we mustn't be
unkind—we've only been joking; perhaps your uncle
is the best possible kind of uncle to have.'

Eileen looked doubtful. 'Well, I don't think he can
be, if he was he'd have been married simply years
ago.' She added anxiously: 'You will stay, won't
you?'

'Provided your uncle will let me, my dear.' Cordelia spoke cheerfully making light of her uncertainty.

It was astonishing how quickly the days flew by.
She quickly discovered that Lady Trescombe was

only too glad to leave her granddaughter in her care
for the greater part of the day. They had lunch and
dinner together and sometimes tea, but breakfast they
had alone and provided Lady Trescombe knew what
their plans were, they could do more or less what they
wanted. True, Cordelia supervised Eileen's piano
practice each morning, and they read together for an
hour during the day but otherwise the time was theirs
to do with it as they wished. They walked miles while
Cordelia listened to Eileen's tales of her parents; they
were never ending and she suspected that the child
was homesick for them. She had spent the last year
with her grandmother, going to a local private school
where she had been happy enough but, she confided,
lonely. 'Granny's friends are all so old,' she explained, 'and now I'll have to stay with Uncle Charles
and he'll be old too...'

'Well, not as old as all that,' demurred Cordelia,
'and if he wants me to stay, I'm not old at all, really.
Remember we'll be in a foreign city and there's an
awful lot to see there and school will be fun. Can you
speak any German?'

'A little, we had to learn it at school.'

'Splendid—I can speak it a little too, so we'll have
fun exploring when you're out of school.' She saw
Eileen pout and said hastily, 'Let's make plans for the
shopping I still have to do; now what do you suggest
I buy?'

She had two weeks salary and she intended to
spend almost all she had. Once Eileen was in bed
each evening, Cordelia sat in her room, whittling
down her list of clothes until she decided that she had

done the best she could, so that when, two days before
they were due to leave, Lady Trescombe told her that
Bates would drive her into Guildford so that she
might do her shopping, she knew exactly what she
had to look for. Eileen was to go too and if she saw
anything she liked, said her grandmother, Cordelia
could buy it for her; she was given a roll of notes to
use for this purpose although she didn't think that
they would be spent; Eileen had a great many clothes
and surely had no use for more.

Bates dropped them off in the middle of the shopping streets, arranged to pick them up during the afternoon and drove away and Cordelia, clutching her
purse and with Eileen hanging on her arm, began her
search.

She succeeded very well, considering that Eileen
held matters up from time to time, seeing something
that she simply had to have. But Cordelia, while making no objection to this, took care that they didn't
waste too much time and refused to be side tracked
by her young companion's wish that she should buy
several pairs of highly coloured jeans and a handful
of T-shirts. 'Not quite the rig for a governess,' she
pointed out and went on looking for a cotton skirt
with which she could wear coloured blouses. She settled for a sand coloured one, which Eileen declared
was very dull but which was exactly what Cordelia
had wanted. One or two cotton blouses and some sandals took care of her day by day wants—rather sparse,
but that would have to do. A cotton jersey dress in a
pretty blue would do for travelling and exploring museums and churches and a thin silk jersey dress in

pale pastel shades would take care of any social occasions, although she didn't expect many of those. It only remained to buy a cardigan to match the skirt and a pair of plain court shoes. And by then her money was almost exhausted. There was enough to buy undies and tights from a high street chain store but not enough for a raincoat; she would have to make do with her old one. Perhaps in Vienna she would buy one. The pair of them repaired to the restaurant of the store they were in, ate a good lunch and then browsed around the more expensive shops, where Eileen found exactly the kind of sandals she craved. That they were extremely expensive and unlikely to last more than a month or so, were arguments Cordelia tried in vain; they were bought, and since they were gaily striped, it became imperative to find jeans and a top to match them. Cordelia, watching patiently while Eileen started to try on these garments, wondered what Lady Trescombe would say when she handed over the remnants of the money she had given her.

She need not have worried; Eileen's grandmother expressed approval of both sandals and outfit, enquired kindly of Cordelia if she had found all that she required for herself and suggested that the evening might be spent in packing. A lengthy business, for Eileen changed her mind a dozen times in as many minutes and when at last Cordelia had packed for her declared that it didn't really matter if she hadn't got all she needed with her; she could always buy anything she wanted in Vienna. Cordelia, starting on her own modest packing, wondered what Uncle Charles would have to say to that.

They were to fly from Heathrow to Munich and Bates drove them there in the early morning. Although they were joining the cruise ship at Passau, Lady Trescombe had explained, they would be met by a hired car at Munich airport and drive there in comfort; she had, she explained further, a dislike of travelling in coaches. 'And I shall not go ashore,' she told Cordelia, 'but I think it would be good for Eileen to see as much as possible; so you will take all the tours with her. I hope the weather will be fine.'

Cordelia was too thrilled at the prospect of going to somewhere as exciting and romantic as Vienna to worry about the weather. She had almost no money, but she had more new clothes than she had had for a long time, she possessed a passport, and whatever the future held, she was about to enjoy a week of sight-seeing beyond her wildest dreams.

The flight was short, less than two hours and they travelled Club class with only a handful of other passengers, so that Eileen, who considered herself a seasoned traveller, was able to point out various landmarks to Cordelia. When they got to Munich airport and had dealt with their luggage and customs, a task undertaken by Cordelia since Lady Trescombe was obviously in the habit of having someone dealing with the tiresome details of travel, a car was waiting for them and whisked them away long before the other travellers had reached the coaches waiting to take them to Passau.

The country was pleasant, not unlike England, and

the day was fine; Cordelia, in the blue jersey outfit
and thoroughly content with her world, patiently answered Eileen's chatter and left Lady Trescombe to
doze until they stopped at Altotting for lunch. The
hotel facing the square in the centre of the picturesque
little town awaited the arrival of the coach load of
passengers for the ship but Lady Trescombe chose to
have lunch in the smaller of the restaurants and before
the coaches arrived they had finished their light meal
and she was back in the car while Cordelia and Eileen
hurried across to the small old chapel opposite the
hotel, to peer inside at the incredible silverwork on
its walls and wish that they could have had more time
to inspect it. But Cordelia had already discovered that
Lady Trescombe, while good natured and kind, disliked having her plans or comfort upset. She urged
Eileen back to the car and they set off once more.

They reached Passau well ahead of the main party
and were on board, settled in their cabins long before
the first of the other passengers arrived. It was a
splendid ship, Cordelia considered and the cabin she
and Eileen shared was not only roomy, it was comfortable and airy and they had a splendid view from
their large window. Lady Trescombe, next door, had
a double cabin to herself, and presently Cordelia unpacked for her, listened carefully to that lady's plans
for the cruise, bade Eileen stay where she was for the
moment and went to the reception desk to deal with
Lady Trescombe's wishes. They weren't many but
they were exacting and at the same time, she took a
quick peep round the ship; the restaurant, the lounge,

the sundeck and swimming pool. It all looked very satisfactory.

She was to book any tours which Eileen fancied, she had been told and Lady Trescombe had given her sufficient money to pay for them all and buy any small things she or Eileen needed. She, herself intended spending a quiet time reading and resting and she made it plain that although the pair of them might enjoy themselves as much as they wished, she didn't want to be unduly disturbed. Which suited Cordelia well enough; she and Eileen spent half an hour deciding where they would go ashore, then they explored the ship, inspected the swimming pool and went back to their cabin to get ready for the evening.

The Captain's cocktail party, they had been told, was to take place before dinner. The three of them went along to the lounge, Lady Trescombe in a simple black dress which had probably cost more than the whole of Cordelia's wardrobe put together. Eileen in an equally expensive outfit and Cordelia in one of the jersey dresses. The lounge seemed very full of people; Lady Trescombe sat herself down at once but Cordelia and Eileen, glasses of some drink or other in their hands, found themselves caught up in a cheerful group of passengers. It was a pity, thought Cordelia that they weren't sharing a table with one or two other people, but Lady Trescombe, while perfectly civil to everyone, had no intention of getting involved in any but the most transitory of conversations. The three of them dined at a window table and since by then it was quite late, went to their cabins afterwards.

The sound of the river water under their window

was very soothing, Cordelia was asleep within minutes of putting her head on the pillow.

The pair of them were up early and up on deck before many of the passengers were awake. It was chilly but fine and they hung over the side admiring the magnificent scenery, planning their day. They were to go ashore and see the little town of Durnstein after lunch and a good part of the morning would be taken up with getting tickets for their various trips ashore. And since everything was strange and the scenery changed at every bend of the river, Cordelia thought it unlikely that Eileen would be bored.

They went down to breakfast presently; Lady Trescombe had declared that she would breakfast in her cabin and didn't wish to be disturbed until after that; they ate their meal unhurriedly, exchanging small talk with the occupants of the tables nearby while Eileen speculated about her stay with Uncle Charles.

The child was worried guessed Cordelia, and did her best to calm her down a little. 'Look Eileen,' she coaxed, 'would it be a good idea to forget your Uncle Charles until we get to Vienna? There's such a lot to do before then. I don't believe he'll be half as bad as you think.'

Eileen frowned. 'It's all very well for you, Cordelia.' She tossed her head. 'Mummy says I'm a high spirited child and mustn't be thwarted; I bet Uncle Charles thwarts me.'

'Why should he? And you're not going to be there for ever, you know.'

'If he won't let you stay, I shall run away.'

'In that case, I'll have to stay, won't I?' Cordelia

sounded matter-of-fact. 'Now let's stop worrying about something which I'm sure won't happen. Suppose you get out your camera and get some photos taken? We can have them developed when we get to Vienna and stick them in an album then you can show them to your Mother and Father.'

Durnstein, when they reached it, was a small picturesque town crowned by the ruins of the castle where Richard the Lionheart had been held captive and found, finally, by the faithful minstrel, Blondel. The pair of them wandered through the narrow mainstreet, speculating about the horrors of being held captive in a draughty old castle on the top of a hill for years on end until they did find a small shop crammed with enamel ware and embroidery where they browsed happily for half an hour before going back on board.

The days were much the same although the places they visited were different. Bratislava they found disturbing and Cordelia was sorry that they had gone ashore. The man on duty at the gangway with a gun slung over his shoulder was disconcerting, especially as he neither answered their polite greeting or smiled, and there was nothing to buy. But it gave Cordelia a good reason for delving into modern history and explaining intricate facts like European boundaries, until now she hadn't felt that she was earning her salary and it was a pleasant surprise to find that Eileen was really interested.

They were to go to Budapest before they went ashore at Vienna, and here Lady Trescombe declared her intention of joining them. There was a taxi waiting for them and presumably someone had told the driver where to go for they crossed the Danube and drove up a winding road to an ancient citadel crowned by the statue of a woman. 'Symbolising freedom,' explained Cordelia to Eileen, having taken the trouble to read it all up beforehand.

They inspected the Matthias church next and Fisherman's Bastion, exploring avidly until Lady Trescombe, professing herself already worn out, decided that they should go to the nearby Hilton Hotel and have their coffee. After that, since someone had mentioned that there was a shop close by where they might find some embroidery, they bade the patient cabby wait and found their way there. The shop was in a cellar, stuffed to overflowing with the kind of things tourists would want to buy. Eileen immediately demanded an embroidered blouse, which her grandmother allowed her to buy while she bought a pair of charming little figurines. But Cordelia didn't buy anything for the simple reason that there was no one to whom she might give it. She was tempted by the boxes of painted eggs, but they looked fragile and since her future was uncertain, there seemed no point in buying them.

They went back presently and the taxi took them back across the river into the modern part of the city and here Lady Trescombe paid off the driver and declared herself ready for lunch. The hotel was modern but once inside it revealed an unexpected charm. White walls rose on all sides to the roof in a series of balconies, festooned with ivy. They sat at a little table and drank iced squash and then lunched in the

splendid restaurant. Cordelia enjoyed every minute of
it.

They went back to the boat presently and Lady
Trescombe went straight to her cabin to rest and enjoy
a tray of tea, but Cordelia and Eileen went to hang
over the rails, pointing out to each other the various
landmarks they remembered from the morning.

'If Vienna is half as nice,' declared Cordelia, 'it
will be super.'

She packed for them both that evening for they
would arrive by midday the next morning, and after
breakfast she packed for Lady Trescombe too.

'You have enjoyed the trip?' asked Lady Trescombe, 'Eileen has been a good girl?'

'Oh, yes, Lady Trescombe, I've loved every minute, and Eileen has been quite splendid; she's been
interested in everything too; it will help her with her
school lessons and after Budapest she's looking forward to exploring Vienna.'

'I'm glad to hear it. Certainly you have made a
good companion for her—she can at times be a very
difficult child, but you get along well, I believe.
Surely I shall recommend most strongly that you stay
with her at her uncle's house until her parents return.
Unless of course, you wish to return to England?'

Cordelia couldn't say no fast enough, to that.

They disembarked as soon as the formalities were
dealt with. Cordelia and Eileen had made a few
friends during their days on board; they bade them
goodbye, suddenly reluctant to leave the familiar
faces of the last few days, and followed Lady Trescombe down the gangway. There was a dark blue

Jaguar car parked close by with a discreet GB on its back. Standing beside it a portly man of middle height, dressed soberly in a blue suit. Cordelia's first idea that it was Uncle Charles was dispelled when she saw the peaked cap in his hand and heard Lady Trescombe say with satisfaction: 'Ah, there is Thompson with the car—Charles remembered.'

She greeted the man, introducing him to Cordelia and Eileen before getting in and settling herself on the back seat. 'You may sit with me,' she told Eileen. 'Be good enough to sit beside Thompson, Miss Gibson.'

To start with the streets looked uninteresting but then what could one expect? Dock areas all looked alike and neglected somehow, but presently the street opened into a wide boulevard and Thompson murmured: 'The Ring, Miss, runs right round the centre of the city and very famous.'

The buildings had become large and grand and there were little corners of green and trees. Museums, Cordelia guessed, and then large apartment houses with heavily curtained windows which concealed who knew what splendours within. They gave way presently to shops, very elegant too, this would be the Karntner Ring that Lady Trescombe had mentioned one day, and these in turn made way for vast buildings which had to be more museums or perhaps government offices, and then a sweep of green fronting that could only be a palace. There were broad avenues running across the grass and stationed on them small open carriages, their drivers in bowler hats and a pair of horses standing between the shafts. But Thompson

went on his sedate way, past the Parliament Building
to turn to the right at the end of the small park facing
it. The street was quiet after the bustle of the Ring
and the stone-faced buildings on either side of it had
an opulent air.

Thompson slowed the car and stopped before a
large mahogany door in the centre of such a building,
he got out, opened the door for Lady Trescombe and
Eileen and then did the same for Cordelia.

He rang the old fashioned bell, observed that he
would see to their luggage, and went back to the car
as the door was opened. The hall porter who had answered the bell wished them good day in his own
language and led them across the elegant lobby to the
lift, ushered them into it and took them to the second
floor. The lobby here was as opulent as the entrance
and there were only two doors in it, facing each other.
He trod magestically across to one of them, rang the
doorbell and waited until the door was opened before
taking leave of them, presumably to help Thompson
with the luggage, and all without almost any words
at all, a situation quickly remedied by the little plump
woman who held the door invitingly open.

'There you are, Madam dear, here at last, and Eileen with you too.' Her beady dark eyes studied Cordelia before she smiled at her. 'And this is the young
lady the doctor mentioned. Come along in,' she stood
aside as they went into the hall, 'I'll let him know
that you are here—stayed home from hospital on purpose to welcome you, he did...' She paused for breath
and one of the doors in the hall was opened and a
man came out.

Uncle Charles, but not the Uncle Charles of her and Eileen's fancy—this man, while no longer young, was still in his thirties and his dark hair was barely touched by grey. He was, thought Cordelia, quite out of her depth, incredibly handsome in a craggy way, and very large, towering over them all in a rather off putting fashion. Oh, how very nice, she thought inadequately and waited for him to speak.

He had a quiet voice and rather slow; she couldn't catch what he said to his mother as he stooped to kiss her before turning to Eileen, standing beside her and staring at him with frank surprise.

His, 'Hullo, Eileen. You don't remember me, do you? I hope you will be happy here until your parents return,' was uttered in a somewhat absent minded way, and Cordelia noticed that he held a book in one hand, one finger marking the place. A pity if he was an absent minded scholar who preferred books to people, she mused and then coloured faintly as Lady Trescombe said: 'This is Miss Gibson, Charles, Eileen's companion.'

'How d'you do,' asked Cordelia politely. The doctor studied her carefully, 'Mrs Thompson shall take you to your rooms,' he said at length, 'we shall be in the drawing room when you are ready. I daresay you would like a drink before lunch.' He nodded at her and took his mother's arm and led her across the hall to another door, opened it and went inside with her, closing it behind him.

'He's awful,' whispered Eileen and caught Cordelia's hand in hers.

'No, dear. I think perhaps he's used to living alone

and isn't quite sure what to do with us.' She didn't say more because Mrs Thompson had come to take them to their rooms.

It was a large apartment; they mounted half a dozen shallow stairs and went down a long passage, thickly carpeted, with Mrs Thompson leading the way, talking cosily all the while. 'Side by side, you are,' she told them, 'and there's a bathroom for you to share. The doctor's along the other corridor and Thompson and I are at the end of his corridor. He thought you'd like to be on your own...'

She opened doors as she spoke, revealing two rooms, furnished very similarly in a rather heavy fashion. There was a connecting door and a view of the street below from their windows. 'Of course,' the doctor only rents this place,' explained Mrs Thompson, tweaking a bedspread into exact lines, 'he doesn't care for it overmuch, but it's handy for the university and the hospitals, and we'll be going home in a couple of months.' She beamed at them. 'Well, I'll leave you to tidy up. You can find your way to the drawing room? If you want any help with unpacking just you ring. I'll be in Lady Trescombe's room putting her things to rights...'

Left alone Eileen looked at Cordelia. 'I'm not going to like it here,' she said defiantly, and peeped at her to see what she would say.

'Well, I don't see how you can say that until we've been here for at least two or three days,' said Cordelia matter-of-factly. 'I thought it all looked rather exciting as we drove here, didn't you? That Palace and those dear little carriages...we might take a ride...'

'All the same,' began Eileen, but Cordelia didn't give her the chance: 'The thing is,' she went on calmly, 'now we're here, wouldn't it be a good thing to sample some of the things we've been reading about on board; I'd love to see the Schonbrunn Palace and eat a cream cake at Sacher's Coffee House and to go to the Spanish Riding School.'

She could see Eileen wavering but she was far too wise to say more. 'Let's tidy ourselves and have that drink,' she suggested.

Five minutes later they were ready. They were on the last stair of the steps leading to the hall and about to cross the hall to the half open drawing room door when Dr Trescombe spoke, his deep quiet voice nevertheless very clear.

'By all means let her stay,' he sounded bored, 'I'm sure that I can rely on your opinion, Mother. I can't say I have felt much interest—a rather dull girl, I should have thought, with no looks to speak of...'

Cordelia had stopped, rooted to the spot, her face had paled and her gentle mouth was half open. She might have stayed there for heaven knew how long but Eileen caught her by the hand and whisked her silently back up the steps. Safely on the landing she whispered fiercely: 'Don't believe a word of it Cordelia, you're not a bit dull and when you smile you're beautiful. I hate him.'

Cordelia managed a smile. 'At least I'm to stay.' She breathed the words into Eileen's ear. 'But don't hate him—he's quite right, you know.'

Eileen scowled and Cordelia put a finger to her lips and urged her down into the hall again. She said in a high and rather loud voice: 'I daresay most people living in Vienna have apartments, I remember reading...'

They had reached the drawing-room door, which was a good thing because she had no idea what she was going to say next.

Lady Trescombe was sitting in an over upholstered chair, a glass on the small table by her side. She said unnecessarily: 'There you are. Eileen, you may have a glass of lemonade. Miss Gibson, you would probably like a glass of sherry.'

The doctor was standing at the other end of the room, looking out of the window. He turned to look at them as they went in but apparently he had no objection to his mother taking over his duties for he said nothing before resuming his study of the street outside.

'I shall return home in two days time,' observed Lady Trescombe. 'You will arrange that for me, Charles? A morning flight I think.'

Cordelia and Eileen had sat down side by side on a massive sofa and he came to sit in a chair opposite his mother.

'Certainly, my dear, although I should have liked you to stay for longer.'

He transferred his gaze to Cordelia and she was startled to see how very blue his eyes were. 'You will remain, Miss Gibson? Eileen's parents will return in rather less than six weeks and I must depend upon you to keep her occupied and happy until then. You must understand that I have my work which keeps me busy and I have little leisure. Your duties are unlikely to be onerous. I have arranged for Eileen to attend a school while she is here,' and at the girl's interruption: 'Don't worry, Eileen, you will only go to the classes you will enjoy. You like painting and drawing don't you? You may go three times a week to art class, and perhaps you might like the cookery sessions and the embroidery... Anyway, try them out, and if you don't like them, we'll think of something else. Your mother wrote to me and suggested it and I know it would please her, but if the idea of school makes you unhappy, we'll scrap it.'

Cordelia found this to be a very reasonable arrangement and was relieved to see Eileen's face brighten. 'I can really choose for myself?'

'Of course. There will be plenty of time for you and Miss Gibson to explore Vienna—feel free to go where you like, provided you let Thompson or Mrs Thompson know where you are going.' He smiled suddenly and looked years younger. 'I'm afraid I'm not much of an uncle, my dear, you must forgive a middle-aged bachelor.'

'Probably,' said Eileen, 'when Cordelia and I have been here for a week or two, you'll feel much younger.'

His eyes flickered over Cordelia. 'Er—quite possibly. Perhaps the two of you would like to unpack?'

Cordelia got up and walked to the door without saying a word, reminding herself that after all he wasn't any worse than her stepmother, and she was being paid for it. As she waited for Eileen she did a little rapid mental arithmetic—five weeks at the salary she was getting, if she saved most of it, would cushion her nicely against the uncertain future.

She had, while they had been on board, spent some time in deciding what she would buy once they were in Vienna, her wardrobe was, after all meagre, but now she realised that half a dozen sacks would do just as well as far as Uncle Charles was concerned and she wasn't likely to make many friends. She would be able to manage very well with what she had.

The pair of them unpacked while Eileen discussed her uncle.

'It's not polite to talk about him when we're guests under his roof,' reproved Cordelia.

'Well I don't think I like him, I expect he thinks we're a nuisance...'

'Quite likely. You see he lives alone and has only had himself to consider. I'm quite sorry for him—I daresay he's a very lonely man.'

Eileen, under Cordelia's direction, was laying shoes and slippers in a neat row in the clothes closet. 'Well, he can get married.' She turned to look at Cordelia. 'I don't suppose you fancy him?'

'No,' said Cordelia, 'I don't think I do, and isn't that a good thing for I don't suppose I'd make much headway, would I?'

They giggled at the very idea, finished their unpacking and went downstairs again.

Lunch was ready as they reached the hall, delayed for half an hour so that Dr Trescombe could talk to his mother. They ate it in a sombre heavily furnished room, sitting spaced out round an oval table. The doc-

tor was a good host; he included Eileen and Cordelia
in the conversation and was attentive to their wants,
all the same Cordelia was relieved when they went
back to the drawing room for their coffee, and presently she gave a speaking look to Eileen and carried
that reluctant young lady off to her room.

'Are you going back to the drawing room?' she
wanted to know as Cordelia prepared to leave her.

'Me? Heavens no. Your grandmother and uncle
will want to talk together.' She could imagine the
polite conversation they would maintain if she were
foolish enough to rejoin them, concealing their impatience with well-bred courtesy. 'I shall go to my
room for a bit, presently I should think we might go
out and take a look round. There's a park close by,
unless your grandmother or uncle want you...'

She left Eileen with a book and went along to her
own room and did her face and hair again for something to do and then went and sat by the window and
watched the street below. She hoped that Uncle
Charles wasn't going to dislike her, it was disheart-
ening that he had such a poor opinion of her, but
perhaps that wasn't such a bad thing; he'd be more
likely to ignore her. And in the meanwhile, here she
was in Vienna, living in what to her was the lap of
luxury and with untold museums, monuments and
palaces to explore. Money to spend too, although she
would have to save most of it.

An hour, she judged, seemed a suitable period in
which to leave mother and son together; she went
through the connecting door to Eileen's room, cast a
critical eye over her appearance, and suggested that

it might be a good idea to find Lady Trescombe and discover her plans for the rest of the day.

An unnecessary exercise, as it turned out for Mrs Thompson knocked on the door with the request that Miss Eileen should go down to the drawing room to her grandmother, and Miss Gibson was asked to go at once to Dr Trescombe's study.

A gloomy, book-lined apartment, she discovered, with dark green curtains draped on either side of the big window and a wide desk set at an angle to the door. The doctor sat behind it, but he got up as she went in and offered her one of the stiff little leather armchairs opposite the desk.

This done, he went to the window and rather impatiently pulled back the curtains so that there was more light in the room. It fell on to Cordelia's face but she didn't turn away from it: in fact she was a practical girl and he'd already decided that she had no looks…

He studied her in a detached way for a few moments. 'My mother tells me that Eileen likes you, a sufficient recommendation for you to remain here. But I cannot stress sufficiently that you must take sole charge of her; I have had very little to do with children and my work precludes my participation in an active social life. I leave you to decide what is suitable for Eileen's entertainment and rely upon you to keep her suitably occupied.'

'In short, Dr Trescombe, you don't want to be aware that we are here.' Cordelia spoke quietly in a matter-of-fact voice but the doctor's eyebrows rose.

'You put it rather more frankly than necessary, Miss Gibson, but yes, that is what I wish.'

'I shall do my best,' observed Cordelia calmly, 'but of course Eileen is a high spirited child, to keep her quite silent will be difficult.'

'I am not an ogre,' said the doctor sharply. 'I shall expect you to come to me if you need help of any sort and naturally, I wish Eileen to be happy while she is here.' He sat back in his chair and said in a more friendly voice. 'You will both take your meals with me; I am seldom home for lunch, but I hope that you will both join me for breakfast and dinner. Occasionally I have guests, and probably it may be better if you and Eileen dine alone—the talk is usually in German.'

Cordelia decided that it was unnecessary to tell him that she knew something of that language. And anyway, Lady Trescombe may have mentioned it. She quite understood that neither Eileen nor herself were likely to add much sparkle to a dinner party and she agreed without hesitation.

'In which case, I don't need to keep you any longer, Miss Gibson. I believe my mother wishes to drive to the shops with Eileen and give her tea at Sacher's. If you care to go out and find your way around for a short time? Mrs Thompson will give you your tea when you return. We dine at eight o'clock.'

He got up and went to open the door for her. Nice manners, thought Cordelia, once more in the hall, but what a waste; head buried in his books when he's not examining his patients. I believe he's scared of having us here. Afraid that we'll upset his bachelor life. She went to her room, dabbed some more powder on her nose, tucked her handbag under her arm and left the house, having been informed by Thompson, hovering in the hall that Lady Trescombe and Miss Eileen had gone off in a taxi. He smiled at her very kindly and pressed a map of the city into her hand before she went. 'I've marked this building with a cross in ink, Miss,' he advised her, 'if you miss your way all you need to do is get a taxi and show the driver the map.'

She thanked him, much cheered by his thoughtfulness, and set off in the direction of the ring. From a hasty look at the map, she saw that provided she kept to it, she would eventually get back to the doctor's apartment, for the Ring encircled the inner City and was clearly marked.

She paused uncertainly on the edge of the pavement, deciding whether to go left or right, and the doctor, watching her from the window of his study, smiled as she turned briskly to the left, where in the distance, she could see the reassuring bulk of the houses of Parliament.

CHAPTER THREE

RETURNING AFTER a brisk hour's walk, Cordelia felt that she had done rather well; guided by the map she had found her way back to the Imperial Palace, conveniently surrounded by museums, the Spanish Riding School and some charming gardens. A good jumping off ground upon which to base the daily excursions she had planned for Eileen.

Back at the apartment, Thompson appeared silently beside her as she went down the hall. 'I will put tea in the small sitting room, Miss. Would ten minutes suit you?'

She beamed at him. 'Oh, Thompson, how nice. Yes, that will be fine. Where's the small sitting room?'

He indicated a door at the end of the hall. 'I rather fancy that will be the room set aside for the use of yourself and Miss Eileen during your stay,' he told her. 'Anything you require, Miss, if you would ask me or Mrs Thompson.' He added poker faced: 'The Dr is much occupied with his work and doesn't wish to be bothered with matters which Mrs Thompson or I can deal with.'

'I understand Thompson, Miss Eileen and I will do our best not to disturb him. I—I was told that he was a very busy man.'

'Indeed, Miss. Writing a book, he is, as well as

lecturing at the medical school and working as a temporary consultant at the general hospital not very far from here, just off the Wahringer Strasse. A kind of exchange of eminent medical men, I understand.'

She found a nicely arranged tea tray waiting for her, with small sandwiches, sugary cakes and tea in a delicate china pot. Uncle Charles might not like his bachelor peace invaded, but he was a thoughtful host. She occupied the hours after that in making out a timetable of their days; it had to be largely guesswork because she wasn't sure for how long each day Eileen would go to school, but with the small guide book she had purchased when she was out, she could see that there were more than enough places of interest to keep them fully occupied for weeks. They would visit the nearby museums first, she decided and heaven knew there were enough of them and there were even more churches... And an odd morning window shopping might be a good idea, and one or two concerts. Well pleased with herself, she looked up as Eileen knocked on the door and came in.

'I've had such a gorgeous tea, enormous cream cakes—it's a super place, Cordelia, I shall take you there, and we looked at some shops and Granny says I may have a new outfit for when Mummy and Daddy get back. I'm to ask Uncle Charles for the money... What have you been doing?'

And when Cordelia outlined her plans: 'It sounds dreadfully dull. I shall tell Uncle Charles that I don't want to visit a whole lot of stuffy museums.'

'By all means,' agreed Cordelia equably. 'I've no doubt that you'll enjoy school better.'

'I won't go to school either. Granny allows me to do as I like.'

'That's nice for you, but of course you'll grow up without two ideas in your head which would be very boring for your friends; young men like to air their views, but you know they like an intelligent listener too.'

'How do you know?' asked Eileen rudely.

'You learn about these things as you grow up,' observed Cordelia calmly. 'But it's up to you, of course. Your uncle won't want me to stay, and quite right too—he'd be wasting his money.'

She wasn't prepared for Eileen's instant reaction to this.

'You're not to go—I want you to stay here with me. If I ask Granny she'll make you stay.'

'No one can make me stay, my dear. I don't want to go, but I quite see that it would be a frightful waste of your uncle's money to keep me here unless I made some effort to improve your mind.'

Eileen smiled suddenly. 'Darling Cordelia, do stay. I promise you I'll go to all the beastly museums you want. I don't want to go to school, but I suppose I'll have to go to those classes Uncle Charles has arranged.'

'I expect you will, but they'll only take up a part of each day, you know. I thought that once a week at least we'd take ourselves off to the shops and have a good look round. You shall help me buy a dress— I'm hopelessly unfashionable.'

'Yes, you are, but you'd look quite pretty if you got a smart outfit. Have you a lot of money to spend?'

Cordelia laughed. 'Almost no money at all, which will make it all the more fun. Now let's get ready for dinner, shall we?'

They went downstairs presently, the best of friends, Eileen in a dress far too elaborate for her age, and Cordelia presenting a neat and unassuming appearance which did nothing for her at all, except to make her look as much like an old fashioned governess as it was possible to be.

Lady Trescombe was in the drawing room, elegant in black chiffon and her son was with her; he was in a dinner jacket and Cordelia instantly felt hopelessly unsuitably dressed, a feeling only slightly mitigated by his: 'I have to go to a reception directly after dinner.' He spoke kindly but with an aloof air which chilled her. Even the glass of sherry she was given before they went into the dining room didn't dispel her gloom.

Dr Trescombe certainly lived in some style; the table was a splendid sight with its starched white linen, gleaming silver and shining crystal. The food matched it; lobster soup, filleted trout, *boeuf en croûte* and a delicious concoction of ice cream and fruit and shredded chocolate topped with whipped cream, made specially, the doctor informed his niece, in honour of her arrival. Cordelia, a little too thin in any case, and not one to put on weight easily, ate everything with a healthy appetite. The job had its drawbacks, she thought, listening to the doctor and his mother discussing the current performance at the Opera House, but it also had its advantages. She hadn't had such a delicious meal for years.

They had their coffee in the drawing room, she had barely set her cup and saucer down when the doctor said carelessly, 'You would no doubt like to see Eileen to her bed, Miss Gibson. If there is anything either of you require will you ask Mrs Thompson? I breakfast at half-past seven. You will be called in good time in the morning.'

Cordelia gave him a clear, faintly pitying look. Good manners wouldn't allow him to show his unease at having them in his house and she would have to make things as easy as possible for him while they were there. She got up at once, waited while Eileen said good night to her grandmother and uncle and added her own quiet 'Good night' and ushered a silently protesting child from the room.

'I don't want to go to bed,' declared Eileen the moment they were in the hall. 'Granny lets me stay up as long as I like.'

'It's very kind of your uncle to have us here,' observed Cordelia matter-of-factly, 'and remember, it's because your grandmother needs a rest. The least we can do is do as he wishes. It's not all that early either, by the time you've had a bath it'll be ten o'clock. Remember we have to be up early in the morning too. Unless your uncle has any special plans for you, I thought we might go along to the Imperial Palace. I walked there this afternoon and it looked well worth a visit. We might take a ride in one of those dear little carriages too.'

This happily had the effect of putting Eileen in a good humour again; she went to bed without further ado and Cordelia was free to go to her room next door.

The curtains had been drawn but she opened the french window they covered and stepped on to the narrow balcony. The street below was brightly lit but quiet, but she could hear the steady hum of traffic in the distance and see the lights of the city all round her. It would be fun, she mused wistfully, to be driven through the streets, past the cafés, and watch the people in them; friends and lovers, husbands and wives, elderly gentlemen sipping whatever it was one sipped in Vienna. Of course, she would need a companion, someone who would listen to her comments and answer her questions... 'Daydreams,' said Cordelia, severely, and turned to go through the window again. She paused at the sound of a car and leaned over the wrought iron railing to watch the Jaguar which had met them at the boat slide to a halt before the house and Thompson get out. A moment later the front door opened and the doctor came out, the lights from the hall silhouetting him against the dark outside. He stood a minute, talking to Thompson and then went unhurriedly to his car. With his hand on the door he turned round and looked back over his shoulder at Cordelia, a small dark figure lighted from the open window. He stared up at her for a long moment and she stared back, wondering if she should call another good night. She was glad that she had decided against that, for he said nothing at all but got into his car and drove away.

She got ready for bed, a little worried that he might have thought that she was snooping, but since there was nothing to do about it, she put her sensible head on the pillow and went to sleep.

A strapping young woman brought her tea in the morning and Cordelia tried out her German on her with quite satisfactory results. When the girl had gone, she got out of bed and peered between the curtains. It was a fine morning and the fresh green leaves on the trees planted on the small grassy plot at the corner of the street rustled gently in the light wind.

Cordelia made sure that Eileen was getting up and got herself dressed in her sensible neat clothes, made up her face without a great deal of interest, brushed her soft hair into smoothness and went to see if Eileen was ready. She wasn't, of course, it took Cordelia several minutes to find the particular T-shirt Eileen simply had to wear so that they only just made it to the dining room with seconds to spare.

The doctor was already at table, but he rose as they joined him, offered a cheek for his niece's kiss, wished Cordelia a polite good morning, and became immediately immersed in the papers scattered round his plate. He wasn't a tidy man, which surprised her, for he presented an immaculate appearance, for as he finished with one letter or the other, he cast them on to the floor beside his chair. He ate what was on his plate when he remembered and she was sure that he wasn't eating nearly enough. The wish to tidy up his correspondence, put a knife and fork in his hand and tell him to eat up was very strong, but she suppressed this motherly instinct and got on with her own breakfast. She had warned Eileen not to talk unless her uncle opened a conversation, so the three of them sat there, not saying a word until at length he threw his napkin to join the papers on the floor and got up, still reading. He had quite obviously forgotten that they were there, indeed, he went through the door without pause and then, to their surprise, poked his head round the door and wished them a pleasant day rather in the manner of a man who had just remembered some small forgotten chore.

'Why doesn't he talk?' Eileen was keen to know, listening to the shutting of the front door.

'I think perhaps he's a very clever man,' explained Cordelia. 'Clever people aren't always aware of the ordinary world around them; they're wrapped up in whatever they're clever about.'

Eileen's eyes gleamed with mischief. 'I say, Cordelia, darling, shall we do something about it? If we could find a beautiful lady in gorgeous clothes to catch his eye.' She studied Cordelia, 'It's a pity,' she said regretfully, 'but I'm afraid that you wouldn't do...'

'No, well, of course I wouldn't,' agreed Cordelia seriously. 'I haven't any gorgeous clothes for one thing, and no one has ever considered me beautiful. But it would be nice if your uncle were to meet someone...it's such a waste, if you see what I mean.'

And Eileen, a precocious child, saw.

Lady Trescombe always breakfasted in her room; there was no hurry, the two of them sat over their meal, planning their morning, always providing Lady Trescombe hadn't already made plans of her own. Which she hadn't. Eileen going to wish her grandmother good morning presently, was told to send Cordelia to her, and when Cordelia tapped on the door and presented herself in the large, splendidly furnished room set aside for Lady Trescombe's use, it was to be told to take Eileen for a drive along the Ring, give her coffee or chocolate in one of the cafés, and then visit St Stephan's Cathedral. 'And after lunch, which you will have here, I intend taking her to the shops with me. You will be free until we return at tea time, Cordelia. I shall be going back to England tomorrow afternoon. I had wished to leave in the morning, but there was no available seat; I shall probably spend the morning with Eileen and you may do as you wish for an hour or so. Your free time is something you must arrange with the doctor, and you must be prepared to have it when it is convenient.' She smiled kindly at Cordelia. 'You are quite happy to remain here until Eileen's parents return?'

'Yes, thank you, Lady Trescombe. I've made a rough list of the more interesting places to visit, and we can see them at our leisure once I know when Eileen is to go to school.'

Lady Trescombe nodded. 'Of course. Charles will arrange that and let you know.'

If he remembers, thought Cordelia, on her way to the door, to be called back and given a roll of notes. 'For the carriage drive and your coffee.'

'Thank you—I'll keep a careful note of what I spend.'

The drive was fun; the carriage was small and open with two well groomed horses and a cheerful driver in the traditional bowler hat. Cordelia had brought her guide book with her but the public buildings which it

listed were largely overlooked by them both; the
shops and cafés and the people thronging the pavements were far more interesting.

They had coffee and mountainous cream cakes
presently and then, obedient to Lady Trescombe's
suggestion, found their way to St Stephan's Cathedral
where they lingered far too long, so that they had to
take another fiacre back to the apartment, much to
Eileen's delight.

The doctor was home for lunch and he questioned
them politely about their morning.

'Your German is adequate, Miss Gibson?' He
glanced at her briefly, not smiling.

'I think so, Dr Trescombe, at least for everyday
needs.'

He nodded. 'I will let you know as soon as I can
arrange Eileen's lessons.' And that was the sum total
of their conversation. She went out again after lunch
having seen Lady Trescombe and Eileen driving off
in a taxi. She was careful not to go too far and since
it was a warm afternoon, she sat in the Volksgarten,
reading the guide book and making a list of the things
she would like to buy. A fearful waste of time, really,
for she would need to save as much as she could. All
the same, she was conscious that her clothes weren't
adequate; the doctor might be a man wrapped up in
his learned books and papers, but there had been a
decided look of amused scorn in his look when he
had first seen her, thinking of it made her squirm, just
because of that look she was going to buy just one
stunning outfit…

Lady Trescombe and Eileen got back very shortly

after she did and they had tea together while the child enthused about the dress her grandmother had bought her and the splendid shops they had visited, and then, because Lady Trescombe wished to rest before dinner, the two of them went to the small room Thompson had pointed out, and played Demon Patience until it was time to change for the evening. Cordelia put on the dress she had worn previously and then helped Eileen into the vivid printed top and wide skirt she had coaxed out of her grandmother that afternoon. Perhaps, Cordelia thought soberly, it would be a good thing for the child to be away from her doting grandparent for this short time, for she only had to want something to get it. All the same she was a nice child and it was impossible not to like her.

Dinner followed the pattern of lunch with general conversation in which Cordelia was politely included although for most of the time it was of mutual friends and of people the doctor had come to know in Vienna. Of his work he said nothing and she knew that his bland politeness would prevent her from venturing even the mildest enquiry about that. Besides, she reminded herself, governesses and companions and the like were seldom, if ever, treated as one of the family. She owned to being interested in him and strangely sorry for him too. To be so deeply engrossed in his work when he had so much going on around him; probably he didn't know where he was half the time and just as likely, it didn't matter to him.

They drove to the airport at Schwechat after lunch the next day and Cordelia had been surprised to find the doctor at the wheel of the Jaguar. She sat in the back with Lady Trescombe and admired the way he drove; there was nothing even faintly absent minded about the way he sent the car through the crowded streets of Vienna until they had passed the suburbs and after that it seemed no time at all before they were at the airport. She had expected to stay in the car while Eileen and her uncle saw Lady Trescombe through the checking of baggage and bade her good-bye, but Dr Trescombe had told her briefly to go with them and she had done so, feeling like an intruder and thankful that she was an insignificant person capable of melting into the background as necessary. But it had been a wise decision. Once Lady Trescombe had gone through the gate, Eileen had burst into a passion of tears and after one look at the doctor's helplessness, Cordelia had taken charge with her quiet competence, mopping the child's face and talking quietly until Eileen at length stopped weeping. She muttered pathetically. 'I've been with Granny a long time... She's so nice...'

The doctor flung an arm round her shoulder. 'Yes, she is, isn't she? I shall miss her too. But she does need a rest, Eileen, and think what fun it will be when your mother and father get back and we'll all have a big party. You must search the shops here for a really fine present.'

For the doctor a surprisingly long speech and a very understanding one. Cordelia gave him an approving look, offered a clean handkerchief to Eileen and observed, 'I believe the enamel ware in Vienna is famous...'

In the car, sitting in the back once more, but alone

this time, she heard with astonishment, 'I think tea at Sacher's, don't you, Miss Gibson?'

She kept her voice very level. 'It sounds delightful, Dr Trescombe.' So they had tea at that famous coffee house and while the doctor contented himself with a pot of coffee, she and Eileen had their tea in dainty little pots and ate unbelievably large and creamy cakes while they talked cheerfully about everything under the sun, the only thing they didn't mention was Lady Trescombe, by then about to land at Heathrow.

In the small sitting room, an hour later, studying the city's map with Eileen, deciding where they should go the following day, Cordelia hoped that their tea party had been a good augury for future relations between uncle and niece, and me too, she added silently.

Wishful thinking; he was, if anything, more remote than ever at dinner that evening. True, he sustained a conversation in a vague way and answered his niece when she addressed him but Cordelia had the feeling that they were quite superfluous to his entertainment. It was a relief when the meal was finished and politely refusing coffee, she was able to usher Eileen up to her bed and then go along to her room.

They saw very little of the doctor during the next two days, he joined them at breakfast but as on the first occasion, beyond wishing them good morning and bidding them a brief goodbye, he had nothing to say, plainly he preferred to occupy himself at that meal with his correspondence. At lunch he was rather more forthcoming, asking where they had been and where they intended to spend their afternoon, and dinner in the evening was very much the same as lunch. It was on the third morning that he surprised Cordelia by pausing on his way from the breakfast table to ask her if she would be good enough to join him in his study when she had finished her own meal.

He was sitting at his desk writing when she knocked and went in. He got up and pulled a chair forward for her and then sat down again.

'I imagine that Eileen is sufficiently settled to start lessons of some sort?' He asked, barely giving her a glance or a chance to nod her head: 'There is an art class at the school close by, opposite the church of the Scots, a few minutes walk from here. This afternoon at three o'clock. I believe it lasts for an hour. And tomorrow morning she will attend a needlework class at nine o'clock. I have arranged for her to have German lessons three times a week, I presume you are capable of helping her with any homework she may have to do?'

Cordelia nodded again, and spoke quickly before he could say anything more. 'That's all a bit dull for a twelve-year-old,' she pointed out forthrightly. She ignored the lift of his heavy eyebrows. 'How about some gym or tennis; she'd meet some girls of her own age…?'

'And be taken off your hands, Miss Gibson?' His voice was silky.

She reddened up to the roots of her hair. She said in her quiet voice which only shook a little with anger. 'I'm sorry you think that, Dr Trescombe. I am aware that Eileen and I interfere with your life, but it isn't for long. I've tried to work out a daily routine which will keep us out of your way as far as possible, but Eileen is a lively girl and normally quite noisy as well as rather spoilt, but she's a dear child too, and she didn't ask to come here.'

'Plain speaking, Miss Gibson. You must forgive me; as I have said before I have very little to do with children. My world is largely of books and reading.'

She looked at him with pity; still young, handsome enough for any woman to look at him twice, apparently successful and by no means poor. It seemed to her a wicked waste... She looked quickly away because he was staring at her in enquiry. After a moment he said: 'I'll arrange for gym classes and see about tennis. You play yourself?'

Colour stole into her cheeks again. 'Yes, but not for a long time. Besides I have no racket and—and no clothes. I shall enjoy watching her; she can use up some of her energy.'

'You will also take her to the museums and churches. On Sunday I will take her to the Spanish Riding School, and you might visit the Belvedere Palace Gardens and I suppose she will want to go to the shops. Keep to those in Karntner Strasse and the Graben please. I think it might be a good idea if you were to put your suggestions for any outing on this desk from day to day. Have you sufficient money?'

'No,' said Cordelia baldly. 'I gave Lady Trescombe the change from the money I had to take Eileen out.'

He nodded. 'I will advance you a sum for expenses, be good enough to tell me when you need more. Oh, and your wages? Paid weekly, I understand.'

It made her sound like a Victorian servant. She said

stiffly: 'Lady Trescombe paid me each Saturday morning.'

He pulled a pile of papers towards him and picked up a pen. 'Very well, Miss Gibson. I think that is all, thank you.'

She, usually mild tempered and patient, longed to speak her mind; he was as dull as his books and there was absolutely no need for it. He needed a good shaking up; Eileen's idea of finding a beautiful woman to dangle under his uncaring nose wasn't so silly. She went out of the room without a word.

Eileen was waiting for her. 'Well, what was all that about?' she wanted to know.

'Let's go across to the Rathaus Park, we can sit there and talk.'

It was still early in the morning and the streets weren't busy although the traffic was heavy as they crossed the Ring. But the park was almost empty. They found a seat in the sun and Cordelia passed on as much of the doctor's wishes as she deemed suitable and when Eileen, inevitably, complained bitterly, she stressed the pleasures of the tennis and the various outings she had planned. 'The Vienna Woods,' she coaxed, 'and the Schonbrunn Palace, it's huge and the gardens are quite super. Besides your mother and father will expect you to see as much as possible, and I thought it rather a splendid idea for you to have German lessons; you can try out what you learn in the shops and it'll be a lovely surprise—only five weeks.' She added cunningly, 'You'll have to work hard—we can do your homework together, I need to brush up my German too.'

Eileen hunched her shoulders. 'Oh, all right, if you say so. But I don't want to play tennis with a lot of stuffy girls.'

'Well yes I can understand that, but you ought to give it a try or you won't know if they are stuffy or not will you?' She stood up. 'There's a nice little café over there, let's go and have coffee or lemonade or something. Did you bring your paints with you?'

Cordelia began to walk across the park. 'The school's quite near here; while you're at your class, I'll look at a church or two. Tomorrow after your class we might walk to the Graben and look at the shops.'

'What will we do when we've had coffee?'

'We're going to take a look at the Museum of Fine Arts,' said Cordelia firmly.

To her surprise they slid into quite a pleasant routine; the art classes weren't so bad, conceded Eileen, and she had begun on a work bag in typical Austrian style for her mother, and tennis, provided Cordelia sat at the side of the court and watched, was bearable. Cordelia heaved a sigh of relief, exchanged polite small talk with the doctor when they happened to meet which was only during meals anyway and being a methodical girl crossed off the various museums as they visited them.

Of course it wasn't all museums; the doctor had been as good as his word and taken them both to the Spanish Riding School on Sunday morning and they had sat entranced, watching the magnificent horses with their riders in their strange hats and uniform, dancing and trotting and gavotting round the ring. Dr

Trescombe, who had seen it all before, found it far more entertaining to watch his niece's small, excited face and Cordelia's eyes, wide with delight, darting here and there and everywhere. Not so plain, he decided, studying the long curling lashes and the pale hair pinned so neatly. A lot of hair; he wondered just how long it was and what it would look like unpinned and then frowned at the thought, and when she turned to ask him something, answered her with the cool politeness she was beginning to dislike. After lunch, he took Eileen out to meet some friends of his and Cordelia, with time on her hands and not knowing what to do with it, armed herself with her guide book and found her way to the church of the Minor Friars where she sat quietly, watching the constant coming and going of people through its doors. It made her feel less lonely.

In these surroundings it would have been easy to give way to self pity, instead she totted up all the advantages of her job; money—more than she had had for a long time, splendid food and a handsome apartment to live in. A chance to see something of the world at no expense to herself and she hoped, her feet firmly on the first step towards an independent life of her own. Not bad, she told herself bracingly and walked back to the apartment, getting lost on the way.

Thompson opened the door to her as the doctor came from the drawing-room into the hall, and she paused uncertainly as she saw him. She was a little flurried because just for a while she had had no idea where she was despite the guide book and she looked at him uncertainly. All she wanted was a cup of tea and somewhere to sit and if he were to ask her in his chilly way where she had been she might possibly scream...

For all his austere manner, Dr Trescombe was no fool. He said at once, 'Ah, there you are Miss Gibson—I was about to ask Mrs Thompson to send in tea—Eileen and I are parched and I daresay you are too.'

He looked over her shoulder at Thompson. 'So tea, Thompson, if you please, and cucumber sandwiches and some of Mrs Thompson's apple cake.'

Thompson, well aware that both the doctor and his niece only just had returned from having tea with a minor consulate official, went off smartly to the kitchen with a poker face. 'Never known him like it,' he observed to his wife, 'putting himself out and no mistake, not but what Miss Gibson's a very nice young lady, wouldn't hurt a fly and so kind and thoughtful.'

In the hall Cordelia still hesitated, 'I'll be down in a minute,' she told him and went up the steps and along the corridor leaving him to return to Eileen.

'Miss Gibson's just come in, she's hot and tired and we're going to have tea—never mind that we've just had it, we're going to have it again...'

Eileen stared at him frankly. 'You know, Uncle Charles, I think you're rather nice after all. I bet Cordelia's been roaming around feeling lonely, though she'd rather die than say so. She's very proud. She's got almost no clothes and she's always doing little sums in a note book but she'd be angry—no, not angry, just sort of disappear into herself, if I said anything. I know because I've tried.'

Her uncle was on the point of replying to this when Cordelia came in, instead he said kindly, 'Sit down, Miss Gibson, it's almost too hot to be out. I miss a garden, don't you? Did you find somewhere cool while you were out?'

'Well, yes, a little church...' she described it briefly, afraid of boring him and then asked politely if they had had a pleasant afternoon.

'Heavenly,' cried Eileen, chipping in, 'and we had strawberries...'

'The friends we visited have a garden,' interrupted the doctor smoothly, 'they have a villa at Grinzing, one of the fashionable areas in which to live. We must drive out that way one evening.'

Mrs Thompson with a small conspiratorial smile at the doctor, put the tea tray on the handsome sofa table between the windows and Cordelia, bidden by the doctor to do so, poured out. The tea, what Mrs Thompson described privately as a good cuppa, was fragrant in the delicate china cups and the sandwiches were paper thin. Cordelia took a bite and closed her eyes for a second.

'Of what are you thinking?' asked the doctor.

She gave him a clear look. 'That heaven is a cucumber sandwich,' she told him seriously.

His bellow of laughter quite shook her. Suddenly he looked quite different; younger, ready to be amused. It was a great pity that at that very moment Thompson should come in to say that there was an urgent 'phone call for him from the hospital. He went away with a muttered word of apology and didn't come back.

He hadn't returned by dinner time, and Cordelia and Eileen, after an evening spent puzzling over the complicated embroidery she had chosen to do, ate without him. And after another hour making plans for the following day, Eileen agreed to go to bed.

'He's fun,' she confided to Cordelia, 'you wouldn't know that, would you? I mean he's always got his nose in a book or something, but this afternoon he played rounders—those people we went to see have five children—just imagine—and their mother and father played too, and we had a huge tea...' She stopped. 'Oh Lord, that was a secret...'

'Why?' asked Cordelia, and knew before she was told.

'Well, you looked kind of lonely and unhappy this afternoon and I think Uncle Charles felt sorry for you, so he pretended we were just going to have tea so that you could have it too.'

'How very thoughtful of him,' observed Cordelia, if her voice was wooden Eileen didn't notice.

'You won't tell him that I told you?' she asked anxiously.

'No, of course not. I'm glad that you had such a super afternoon. You see it's more fun than you had expected, isn't it?'

Eileen was tugging on her pyjamas and her voice was muffled. 'Oh, yes. But not for you Cordelia—I mean you don't meet anyone do you? Only me and Thompson and Mrs Thompson and Uncle Charles. And you hardly see him at all...'

Cordelia saw him that very evening. With Eileen safely in bed and the doctor from home, it was a good chance to go to the little panelled room lined with bookshelves and choose a book. She had been given *carte blanche* to take anything she wanted from the shelves, but somehow she had never got around to it, but now, with the best part of the evening to fill in before bedtime, she would curl up by her open bedroom window and read.

There was a splendid collection; she browsed for ten minutes or so and decided on *Jane Eyre*; she knew it very nearly by heart, but it would divert her thoughts; she wasn't quite sure why she wanted them diverted or from what, but *Jane Eyre* would do the trick, she felt sure.

She was crossing the hall when the doctor let himself in and she paused to wish him good evening: 'I've borrowed a book—you did say...'

He nodded impatiently. 'Yes, yes, of course. You are surely not going to bed—it's barely nine o'clock.'

'Well, not exactly go to bed.' She explained, 'I thought I would read...'

'In your room?' he sounded surprised.

'Well, yes...'

'Did I not make myself clear that you might use any rooms excepting my study?'

'No, you didn't,' she smiled at him kindly, 'but it doesn't matter—I'm sure you're a very busy man with a great deal to occupy your mind.'

He had shut the door behind him and put his case on a chair. 'Perhaps you would join me when I have a cup of coffee, Miss Gibson, I've had rather a trying evening.'

'Certainly, shall I get Thompson to fetch it? And where would you like it?'

'In the drawing room, I think,' and as Thompson appeared from the kitchen end of the hall, 'We would like coffee, please Thompson and perhaps some sandwiches.'

He swept Cordelia before him and she found herself sitting in a small chair by the window while the doctor wandered around the room with his hands in his pockets. He said suddenly, 'I shall be glad to get home—I find this apartment oppressive, although it's convenient for the hospital.'

'Will you be here much longer?'

'No, I return within a few days of Eileen's parents arriving here. They will go on almost immediately to Scotland, presumably you will go with them.'

'I have no idea.'

'You have other plans? Another job to go to?'

'No—no, I haven't, but I expect I can get one easily enough once I'm back in London.'

'You can, of course, return to your family.' It was a statement more than a question, and since she didn't want him to ask any more questions, she said, 'Of course,' and turned with relief to Thompson, bearing a massive tray with coffee and sandwiches.

The doctor sat down after she had given him his coffee and sandwiches. He ate most of them and she asked, 'You had no dinner this evening?'

'Dinner? No—there was a difficult case—there was no time...'

'I'll get some more sandwiches, you must be hungry.'

She went to the door with the empty plate. 'Buttered toast with just a touch of Gentlemen's Relish and more ham sandwiches?'

She was on her way to the kitchen before he could answer.

Mrs Thompson was sitting at the table drinking tea while Thompson cleaned shoes, in the corner of the kitchen.

'The doctor's had no dinner,' said Cordelia urgently, 'and he's eaten all the sandwiches. I wondered if some toast...and some more sandwiches?'

Mrs Thompson beamed at her. 'You go back, Miss, my husband shall bring them along in a minute or two.'

The doctor ate everything that Thompson brought presently, but then, as Cordelia reminded herself he was a big man and there was a lot of him to nourish. She drank a second cup of coffee, listening with a sympathetic ear to some highly technical talk on the doctor's part. Finally, with the coffee pot empty and all the food eaten, he sat back at his ease.

'I must apologise for boring you, Miss Gibson.'

'I wasn't bored. I found it all very interesting, I had no idea that anaesthetics could be so complicated.' She put the cups and saucers tidily on the tray and got up. 'It was kind of you to invite me to coffee, thank-you, Dr Trescombe. I'll say good night.'

She got up and he got up with her. 'It is I who should thank you, Miss Gibson.' He held the door for her and as she went past him: 'Eileen calls you Cordelia, may I do the same?'

She paused to look up at him. 'Of course you can, Dr Trescombe,' she smiled widely. 'Miss Gibson is so unsuitable, isn't it?'

'Unsuitable?'

'Well, yes. The Gibson girls were noted for their beauty, weren't they?'

She slipped away, up the stairs and whisked along the corridor to her room. Probably he had forgotten that he had called her a nonentity with no looks to speak of, but if he had happened to remember, then she had given him something to think about.

CHAPTER FOUR

IN THE MORNING there was nothing in the doctor's face to show whether he had remembered any of his conversation with his mother on that first day. He was, as usual engrossed in his post and his good morning was uttered with the briefest of glances. Only as he got up to go did he pause long enough to say, 'There is a Strauss Concert next Saturday evening, I will get tickets for it.'

'In the same hall in which the New Year concert is given?' asked Cordelia.

'Why, yes. You like music, Miss—Cordelia?'

'Yes, I do, and so does Eileen. We shall look forward to it Doctor.'

'He called you Cordelia,' declared Eileen when they were alone. 'Why?'

'I daresay he finds it most sensible since you call me that. I think it will be delightful to go to a concert, don't you?'

Eileen shrugged. 'I shall wear the dress Granny brought me. What will you wear, Cordelia?'

Cordelia drank the last of her coffee. 'Well, I think we'd better go to the shops and see what I can find.' She had almost all of three week's salary in her purse, surely there would be something she could afford. 'No expensive boutiques, mind you, it'll have to be a dress I can wear for quite a while without it looking too out-of-date.'

'Oh, Cordelia,' Eileen sounded exasperated. 'You'd look smashing in one of those bright prints with a V neck line that goes all the way down and a tight skirt...'

Cordelia said gravely: 'I don't think I'd feel very happy in something like that, love.'

'Why not? You are nice and curvy, only you can't see that in the dresses you wear.'

'It's nice of you to say so, but I don't think it would be quite me. We'll see if we can find something we both like, shall we?'

They decided on Thursday afternoon for their shopping expedition and filled the days before with classes, German lessons with the rather fierce lady who came three times a week, and with visits to the Museum of Natural History, the Historical Museum and the Imperial Palace Chapel. After that lot, Cordelia decided silently, they both of them deserved a little light diversion.

Of the doctor they saw very little; he joined them at meals, made polite enquiries as to their day's activities, listened patiently to Eileen's chatter and had so little to say to Cordelia that she wondered if he could see her. Not that it mattered, she told herself robustly; she hadn't the slightest interest in him either, a statement which, while quite untrue, stiffened her pride.

Thursday was fine and warm, Eileen, by no means a painstaking scholar, applied herself to her German lesson so earnestly that she was let off ten minutes early and she and Cordelia took a tram to Karntner Ring and began their round of the shops without delay. They had about two hours before lunch—not nearly long enough, declared Eileen, accustomed to stroll round the boutiques with her grandmother and try on anything she fancied. But Cordelia knew very well what she wished to buy and refused to be side tracked by her companion's more sophisticated ideas.

She walked briskly past the smart boutiques and began to comb the big stores. In the third one she found what she wanted; a finely pleated crêpe skirt in a pleasing shade of plum with a matching top, very simply cut with a round neck and full sleeves gathered into tight cuffs. By no means high fashion but guaranteed to pass muster for the next year or so. Besides, it seemed to her to be highly suitable for a companion or governess, and she couldn't see herself doing anything else in the foreseeable future.

Eileen, of course, voted the whole outfit stuffy; a jump suit in bright pink, she suggested, or a patterned garment in violent colours that looked as though someone had been slashing a pair of curtains in the hope of turning them into something wearable. Cordelia, refused to be tempted; she liked the plum two-piece, the price was right and it fitted her person exactly as it should. She bought it and solaced her companion with coffee and cream cakes before they went back to the apartment.

She washed her hair on Friday and did her nails with the new nail varnish she had bought and since on Saturday the doctor bore his niece away after breakfast to meet the children of a married colleague, she was free to experiment with her hair. It took her an hour of painstaking pinning and brushing to decide that it would be best not to change her hair style. The doctor went out for lunch and afterwards, since it was a splendid day she took Eileen to Belvedere Palace gardens, where they roamed happily for a couple of hours. They went by tram, a form of transport Cordelia enjoyed enormously and which she considered good for Eileen, a child very much in the habit of getting into a car and being driven without the small problems of getting tickets and paying fares. As it was, she was beginning to enjoy her tram rides, buying the tickets at any tobacconist's shop and getting them stamped. They still had to sample the Underground but as Cordelia sensibly pointed out, trams or buses were much more interesting in fine weather.

The doctor was still not home when they got back, nor did he come in for tea. They were to dine early before the concert and they went to dress in good time—a good thing, for Eileen almost dressed in one outfit, decided that she wasn't going to wear it after all, and spent a frenzied ten minutes making up her mind what she would wear instead. She finally decided on a blue dress and declared herself ready.

'Not before you've picked up the clothes strewn around the room,' declared Cordelia briskly, 'hung them in the cupboard and shut the doors and drawers.'

'Someone else can do it,' Eileen darted a wicked look at her. 'You can.'

Cordelia sat down on the bed. 'Why?' she asked equably.

'Well—you're my governess...'

'So I am, but I can stop being that whenever I want to.' She glanced at her watch. 'Dinner's in ten minutes, I can go downstairs and see your uncle and tell him I don't want to look after you any longer and really you know there's nothing much you can do about that.'

Eileen flew across the room and caught her by the arm. 'You won't—Cordelia, you won't go away? I was only teasing. I'll pick up every single thing. Honest I will. You don't really want to go?'

'No, of course I don't. I like being here and we get on well together but I meant what I said…'

'You won't go?' Eileen wound thin arms round her neck. 'I'm very fond of you, Cordelia, truly I am. I don't ever want you to go away. When Mummy and Daddy get back I'm going to ask if you can stay.'

Cordelia put a motherly arm round the child. 'Well, love, we'll have to see about that when they get here. In the meanwhile tidy this room and we'll go down to dinner. I expect your uncle is back by now.'

But only just, he was striding through the hall, making for his room as they paused at the top of the stairs. He stopped short when he saw them.

'I'm late; give me ten minutes, will you? Cordelia, get yourself a drink and pour me one will you? Whisky, please. Eileen, that's a very pretty dress…'

'Uncle Charles, Cordelia's got a pretty dress too.'

He barely glanced at her. 'So it is.' He couldn't have seen it; she was sure that if she asked him presently what she was wearing he would have no idea. She went into the drawing room with Eileen and poured her a lemonade and herself a glass of sherry and then she poured whisky into one of the cut glass tumblers.

'He's mean,' declared Eileen pettishly, 'he didn't even look and you're quite pretty this evening.'

'Why thank you, love.' Cordelia's voice was as calmly serene as usual; no one, and that meant Uncle Charles, was going to know how hurt her feelings were. Perhaps governesses didn't have feelings? But surely the modern young woman undertaking the education of the young, had feelings and made no bones about expressing them? I'm living in the wrong century she thought and tossed off the sherry rather too fast.

The doctor was as good as his word, freshly shaven, immaculately tailored, he presented a picture of elegance, what was more, he laid himself out to be an amusing companion. They were all in the best of spirits as they got into the car and drove to the Concert House standing back from the Schubertring. It took a very short time; Cordelia wished it could take longer, for Vienna was looking her best; the trees in full leaf, the evening sky clear and bright and the pavements thronged with people. She was as excited as Eileen as they waited at the entrance while the doctor parked the car and then accompanied them to their seats.

The programme was almost all Strauss; Cordelia, a sentimental girl at heart, sat spellbound and stayed so during the interval when they were regaled with cold drinks. The doctor made very little attempt to talk to her but busied himself pointing out the various people he knew in the audience to his niece and answering

with commendable patience, her endless questions.
The concert over, Cordelia still had very little to say
for herself; her head was full of music and snatches
of dreamlike thoughts. They were crossing the hall
when she asked, 'Are the Vienna Woods very
lovely?'

The doctor smiled faintly. 'Oh, yes. They quite live
up to the music. Before you return to England we
must all go there, it's not far; if the weather is fine
we might take a picnic.'

'Tomorrow?' asked Eileen eagerly.

'Good God, no—perhaps next weekend...'

'Why not tomorrow?' persisted Eileen, 'it's Sunday.'

'And I'm spending it with friends in the country!'
There was something in his quiet voice which stopped
her saying more.

Cordelia, going to say goodnight to Eileen found
her tearful. 'I think he's very unkind,' the child began
as soon as Cordelia got into the room.

'He's always reading or shut up in his study or at
his beastly hospital—we don't matter at all...'

'Now that's not fair.' Cordelia sat down on the bed
and kicked off her shoes, taking the pins out of her
hair. 'We're just back from a lovely evening and here
you are moping. It really won't do, love. Your uncle's
days are filled and he has every right to enjoy his free
time in whatever way he wishes. And he's already
said he'll take us to the Vienna Woods and I don't
think he's a man to say something and not mean it.'

Eileen hunched a shoulder. 'I thought I liked
him...'

'And you do. Come on, cheer up, I think he's been very kind to us.'

'Yes, but it's easy to tell Thompson and Mrs Thompson to look after us, and arrange lessons for me and give us enough money so that we can sight see, but he doesn't bother himself, does he?'

'Why should he?' Cordelia spoke bracingly, 'You're a bit young for him you know and I'm rather dull with no looks to speak of.' She caught Eileen's eye and they giggled together. It didn't hurt so much if she laughed about it, thought Cordelia. 'I tell you what, supposing we go to Schonbrunn tomorrow? We could have an early lunch and have tea there. We can go all the way by tram so it will be easy.'

'Uncle Charles won't mind?'

'I can't think why he should. We'll have a guided tour and take a taxi if he doesn't like us to go by tram!'

She put on her shoes and bundled up her hair, thrusting the pins in haphazardly. 'I'll go now and see what he says, it'll be too late if I leave it till the morning.'

The doctor was in his study, writing and if he was vexed at being interrupted he was too well mannered to show it. He got up and offered Cordelia a chair and asked, with only the faintest trace of impatience, what he might do for her.

'I thought Eileen and I might go to Schonbrunn Palace tomorrow if you've no objection. If we could go after an early lunch? We could have tea there and see the gardens before coming home in the early evening. Do you mind if we take the tram?'

'Not in the least; you're a sensible young woman and you have sufficient German to get around, but take a taxi if there's any waiting about.' He opened a drawer in his desk and took out some notes. 'That should be enough, I think—if you spend more let me know.'

She was still smarting from being called a sensible young woman; she didn't dispute that; it was correct, she just didn't like being reminded of it. She thanked him quietly and got up and wished him good night and found him at the door before her.

'You do not find your duties too arduous?'

Compared with her unending care of her stepbrothers and sisters it was childsplay. 'Not at all thank you. Eileen is a nice child and intelligent for her age.'

'But spoilt...'

'Perhaps. Well, yes, she is, but that'll sort itself out when she goes to school and her parents are home again.'

'My mother indulges her and of course she is an only child.'

And when she didn't reply: 'Well, enjoy yourselves tomorrow. Good night Cordelia.'

'Good night, Dr Trescombe.' She went past him up the stairs and along the corridor to her own room. For no reason at all, she felt unhappy.

Schonbrunn wasn't like anything else she had seen; to begin with it was vast, standing well back from the busy street at its gate. They crossed the vast courtyard, already crowded with visitors and tourists, and went into the courtyard and up the stairs where they joined a small group of people being led around by a guide. Eileen was all for going off on their own, but as Cordelia pointed out, they would get lost in the vastness of the palace, so they tagged along on the fringe of Americans and English ladies in their cardigans, trying to hear what the guide was saying and not miss any of the grandeur around them. Magnificent pictures, portraits of bygone Habsburgs, marvellous painted ceilings, inlaid tables and chairs, damask hung walls—they wandered from one room to the next, trying to take it all in. The Walnut Room, with it's inlaid floor and red Damask, the gloomy bedroom of Franz Joseph the first and his wife, the Yellow Salon, the Hall of Mirrors, the great gallery, where they craned their necks in order to get a view of the painted ceiling. Then they saw the Chinese rooms, a room panelled in lacquer in which, the guide told them solemnly, the Empress Maria Theresa spent her days when she was widowed and which made them both slightly claustrophobic, the Goblin Room, the Napoleon Room, a sad little memorial room of the young Duke of Reichstadt, endless rooms, decked out in red damask, leading from one to the other, affording, as far as Cordelia could see, no privacy. It was all a little more than she could digest and as for Eileen, while admitting that the whole Palace was magnificent, she could see no sense in living in a vast hollow square of huge rooms and said so.

'Yes, but of course, these are the State Apartments, I daresay they had smaller rooms as well,' observed Cordelia. 'It's all very magnificent though, you can just imagine the ladies swishing to and fro in their panniers and silks and satins.'

Just the same she was glad when they reached the final Anteroom and went down the vast staircase and out into the courtyard, and agreed readily enough to go in search of a tea room.

The gardens were a delight, vast and beautifully laid out, with the fountains at the far end. They visited the Roman Ruins, which weren't Roman at all, but built in the eighteenth century. They inspected the dovehouse too and admired the various marble figures but Cordelia drew the line at a visit to the zoological gardens in the park. 'It's too late,' she decided, 'and we can come another day.'

Although Eileen put up a token opposition, her heart wasn't in it; they walked to the gates and since the doctor had been generous, took a taxi back to the apartment.

The doctor was in the hall, bidding goodbye to a woman; not very young but still with striking looks and dressed in the kind of clothes Cordelia longed to possess. The woman looked both Eileen and Cordelia over and dismissed them as of no account, but the doctor wished them a polite good evening. Eileen would have lingered, but Cordelia took her firmly by the arm and urged her into the small sitting room they had come to regard as their own, and shut the door.

'He's got a girlfriend,' hissed Eileen, 'I thought he only read books.'

'Don't be vulgar,' said Cordelia calmly, 'Of course your uncle has friends. I thought she was quite beautiful.'

Eileen eyed her with pity. 'You're too nice, Cordelia: she looked at us as though we were road sweepings. All the same Uncle Charles isn't so bad—I wouldn't like him to marry her, I mean, when he isn't buried in his beastly books or at the hospital, he's quite fun.'

Cordelia didn't answer; she hardly classed as fun the polite conversation they carried on at meals, the brief discussions as to Eileen's well being and the absent minded enquiries as to her progress at her classes. She didn't feel she was qualified to comment.

'How much longer must we stay here?' asked Eileen impatiently.

'Well, we'll hear the front door…' She realised uneasily that they wouldn't, they were too far away. 'I'll take a quick peep,' she decided.

She opened the door cautiously and looked down the hall. The doctor and his visitor were standing where they had left them, the lady with her back to her, the doctor most unfortunately facing her. She met his eyes and closed the door again, which was a pity or she would have seen his smile. 'They're still there,' she said, 'we'll just have to wait.'

She found a pack of cards, got down on the floor with Eileen, and shared a game of Patience with her, they were arguing as to whose turn it was when the door opened and the doctor came in.

'You don't have to shut yourselves up here,' he observed mildly, 'You were free to go into the drawing room or to your rooms.'

'We thought we'd better go somewhere in a hurry, in case you wanted to kiss her,' said Eileen.

'Eileen,' said Cordelia severely, 'You've just made

that up and it was rude. Be good enough to apologise to your Uncle.'

'Did you kiss her?' said Eileen taking no notice.

The doctor sat down on the arm of a chair and said calmly. 'No—some ladies are so beautiful and so exquisitely dressed one hesitates to, er—rumple them.'

'You wouldn't rumple Cordelia,' observed Eileen, 'she's not exquisitely dressed and she's not beautiful either.'

Cordelia blushed. 'Eileen,' she said awfully, 'there is nothing clever in making remarks like that...'

'Well, it's what I think—why shouldn't I say what I think?'

'It sometimes hurts peoples feelings,' said the doctor placidly 'and Cordelia asked you to apologise.'

'Well I'm sorry, but only because I like Cordelia and I quite like you too.'

'Thank you,' said her uncle meekly. 'Did you enjoy your visit to Schonbrunn?'

The next half hour was spent in an exaggerated and not quite truthful account of their afternoon on Eileen's part. All the same Cordelia was pleased to hear that her pupil had learned a good deal of history as well as forming an opinion of the Palace and it's furnishings.

'And you, Cordelia?' asked the doctor, 'you enjoyed it too?'

'Oh, very much. Very grand, just as Eileen says, and not quite to my taste—all that gilding and none of the chairs looked very comfortable, but the paintings were magnificent...I suppose that they felt at home there?'

'I imagine that if you've never lived anywhere different it would be home. I like something much more cosy myself.' He got up and strolled to the door. 'I shall be out this evening. Thompson will look after you. I'll see you at breakfast.'

'I bet he's having dinner with that woman,' said Eileen, and Cordelia rebuking her, agreed silently.

He was at breakfast the next morning, as usual immersed in letters and the daily papers; beyond a brief acknowledgement of their presence, he had nothing to say and he was equally silent at lunch, saying only enough for politeness and then shutting himself in his study. Mindful of his wish for peace and quiet, Cordelia took Eileen for a walk, but the child seemed tired and they found a seat in the park and sat down in the sun. 'What's wrong love?' asked Cordelia, 'you're very quiet. Don't you feel well?'

'I'm all right—I feel sick and I've got a tummy ache.'

'Then we'll go back home and you shall have a rest on your bed—you'll feel better after a sleep. Perhaps you did too much at gym this morning.'

She seemed better after tea although, most unlike her, she showed very little interest in what she should wear that evening, neither did she eat much of her dinner. Cordelia coaxed her to bed early and wondered if she should mention it to the doctor and decided that she would, but when she went downstairs to find him he was gone.

'Back to hospital, Miss,' said Thompson comfortably, 'some patient giving trouble more than like—'phoned him half an hour ago they did.'

Cordelia went back upstairs. Eileen was already asleep; she looked flushed and she felt warm under Cordelia's cool hand; her pulse was rather fast but she wasn't restless. Cordelia went away and had a bath and got ready for bed and then went back to take another look.

Eileen was awake, tossing and turning in a rumpled bed. Cordelia bathed her face and hands, straightened the bedclothes. 'Where does it hurt, love?' she asked worriedly.

'I'm going to be sick,' said Eileen, and was.

Cordelia mopped her up. 'Darling, you've eaten something…'

'My tummy hurts.'

'I'm going to see if your uncle's home, he'll take the pain away. Try and lie still, I'll be quick.'

She flew along the passage and down the stairs and flung open the study door. The doctor was writing at his desk. 'You're back,' declared Cordelia breathlessly: 'Eileen's not well, she's been sick, she's feverish and she's got a tummy ache.'

He went past her almost before she had finished speaking and she rushed after him, to stand by Eileen's bed while he bent over his niece.

'How long has she been like this?'

'She had a headache this afternoon and a tummy ache; she had a nap before dinner and then she came to bed early—she's been asleep…'

He said without looking up: 'Get Thompson, tell him to get the car and bring it to the front. Get some clothes on and wrap Eileen in a blanket. I'm going to

take her to hospital.' He glanced at her then. 'Don't
waste time.'

A needless injunction. She roused Thompson,
threw on a sweater and slacks and went to wrap Eileen in a light blanket. She was just ready when the
doctor came back, picked up his niece and carried her
out to the car. No time to pack a bag, thought Cordelia wildly, I'll have to come back for her things,
and nipped smartly after him, and a good thing too,
for he told her to get into the back of the car and then
settled Eileen beside her. 'Hold her tightly,' he said
brusquely, 'I've given her something for the pain, but
every jolt will hurt.'

She had only a vague idea where the hospital was
and even if she had known it would have been hard
to see where they were going at that hour of night.
She put her arms round the child and held her close,
listening to Eileen's half-conscious moans, praying
that someone would do something quickly.

There wasn't a great deal of traffic; she recognised
the Ring as they crossed it, recognised too the Wahringer Strasse before the doctor turned into side
streets and then thankfully into the forecourt of the
hospital.

He must have telephoned, she thought vaguely, for
there were people waiting for them. The doctor lifted
Eileen out of the car on to the waiting stretcher and
the little group set off through the wide doors with
Cordelia, not sure if she was wanted, in hot pursuit.
At least she wasn't entirely forgotten; at the end of a
long corridor, just before they disappeared through a

swing door the doctor flung 'Wait here,' over his shoulder, then disappeared too.

Cordelia looked about her, there was no one in sight; the corridor had widened itself into a kind of waiting room with a few metal framed chairs against the walls and nothing else. She sat down. Catching her breath, wishing that she knew what was happening. Someone would come and tell her presently, she supposed, in the meantime, she must just sit.

There was a clock on the wall and she was surprised to see that it was already after eleven o'clock. She looked away from it and tried to think back over the day, wondering what Eileen could have eaten— or perhaps it was appendicitis? Whatever it was, the child was ill and in pain. The clock ticked on and Cordelia, in a nightmare of worry and pity and uncertainty, watched the hours slip away.

It was almost two o'clock when the swing door at last opened and the doctor came through. He fetched up before her and said in a voice of whispered thunder. 'What the devil are you doing here? Why haven't you gone home?'

She shook her hair back over her shoulders and eyed him tiredly. 'You told me to wait, and I didn't know how to get home, did I? It's dark outside and I had no money for a taxi even if I had known where to get one and I would have got lost if I had walked. What have you done with Eileen? Is she all right?'

She looked up at him, standing there, not a hair out of place looking as though he'd not done anything in a hurry in his life.

'Eileen is in bed asleep. She has had her appendix removed.'

She got to her feet then. 'Oh, the poor poppet. She's all right? You're sure?'

'Quite sure. I administered the anaesthetic.' There was no conceit in his voice, merely an assurance that nothing was amiss. 'She'll be out of bed later today and home in a week.'

'Can I see her?'

He shook his head. 'She's already asleep—I told you that, besides you're not in a fit state to see anyone. You'll go home and go to bed and in the morning I'll bring you with me—you can pack a few things for her. Come along now.'

They drove back in silence and it wasn't until they were in the apartment that the doctor said, 'Come to the kitchen, Thompson will have left some coffee.'

She had only once before been in the kitchen; it was a nice place, very clean and scrubbed, with rows of saucepans on the wall and a very modern electric cooking stove. She sank down on one of the chairs at the table and watched him fetch the coffee pot from the hob and pour the coffee into the mugs set ready on a tray. He added sugar and cream and handed her one. 'Drink it at once, and then go to bed,' he told her in the kind of voice she had not the least desire to argue with. She did as she was told, wished him good night and took herself off to bed.

'And don't lie awake worrying,' his voice was kind, 'there is no possible blame attached to you, indeed, you did very well... Eileen will be perfectly all right. I daresay they'll be glad to have you spend some time with her—I'll see the sister in the morning. Good night, Cordelia.'

She fell into bed, making a mental list of the things she should take with her to the hospital, and fell asleep in the middle of it.

She got up the moment she was called, showered and dressed and packed a bag for Eileen and presented herself at the breakfast table. Dr Trescombe was already there, exactly as usual, reading his letters and neglecting his breakfast. His good morning was vague and he made no mention of the night's happenings. To her they had been highly dramatic, but she supposed, upon reflection, that to a doctor they were commonplace enough, even when his own flesh and blood were concerned. She wondered if he had telephoned Eileen's parents, but decided not to ask; he was glowering over a closely written sheet and she didn't think he would thank her for interrupting his perusal of it.

She got on with her breakfast and when he said suddenly, 'Well, are you ready? I want to leave in five minutes,' she put her cup tidily in the saucer and said composedly, 'Quite ready, Dr Trescombe' and went and fetched the bag, a couple of books she thought Eileen might like and her own purse, and presented herself in the hall very neat and calm.

The doctor came out of his study, his bag in his hand and paused to look at her. 'You are a remarkably sensible young woman Cordelia—I must admit that I am agreeably surprised at your...'

She interrupted him ruthlessly. 'Should I be flattered? Well, I'm not. Dull young women, with no looks to speak of, don't expect flattery, nor do they like it, let's go.'

She marched to the door to have her arm caught in a merciless grip.

'Well, well,' said Dr Trescombe softly, 'not dull at all and quite an eyeful when she's in a temper. I am surprised, Cordelia.'

'Let go of me, you—you bookworm…'

His great bellow of laughter shook her.

'And don't you dare laugh.' She drew a deep breath. 'And I'm leaving here the moment Eileen is better.'

He didn't answer that, instead he bent his head and kissed her gently. 'You're upset,' he sounded exactly like the family doctor at home, 'We'll talk about it when you feel more yourself.'

She opened her mouth to answer him and then decided not to; she could see that he wasn't going to listen, anyway.

They drove in silence to the hospital and once they were there, the doctor wasn't Uncle Charles any more, but someone important who wasn't going to waste time listening to her. She followed him and a bunch of white coated young men along a corridor and in through swing doors. It was very quiet here and the nurses they met hardly made a sound as they passed, only a faint rustle of crisp cotton. So much nicer than those nylon uniforms at home, she thought and was ushered into a small white walled room, sparsely furnished and Eileen sitting up in bed.

Having her appendix out didn't seem to have made any difference to Eileen; she gave a crow of delight at the sight of her uncle and Cordelia and began to talk. 'I've been out of bed,' she informed them, 'and Sister says I'm a brave girl. It hurts a bit but not when I sit up. Wasn't it exciting? Last night, I mean—I bet you were worried, Cordelia?'

Cordelia bent to kiss a rather pale cheek. 'I have never been so worried in all my life before, love. It's marvellous to see you looking so well.'

She smiled rather mistily at the child and retreated from the bed, because the doctor was standing on the other side and she didn't want to look at him, let alone speak.

She need not have worried, his whole attention was on his niece; he asked her business-like questions, conferred with an elderly man who had slipped into the room just after them, remarked that as far as he could see she would be out and about again in no time at all, bade her be a good girl and went away without so much as glancing at Cordelia.

'You're going to stay?' demanded Eileen, 'It's aw-fully lonely here...'

'Of course I'll stay—just as long as they let me. I've brought you some pyjamas and a few books and odds and ends you might need. If you feel up to it I'll give your hair a good brush and then put every-thing away. I don't suppose you've eaten anything yet?'

Eileen wrinkled her nose. 'Something sloppy for breakfast but I'm to have a proper lunch.'

Cordelia stayed until she was politely asked to leave about noon so that Eileen could eat her lunch

and then rest. 'Come back Cordelia,' Eileen suddenly
sounded very young.

'Of course I'm coming back. About six o'clock Sister says. Mind you speak German as much as possible; it's a splendid chance to improve your vocabu-
lary.' She kissed Eileen and made her way out of the
hospital, glancing at her watch. She could walk back
but it might take rather a long time and she didn't
want to be late for lunch; even if she was going to
eat it alone from a tray in the little sitting room, Mrs
Thompson would have it ready on the dot. She
crossed the courtyard quickly; there were trams in the
street beyond, one of them would surely go in her
direction. She was almost at the gates when the Jaguar
crawled to a halt beside her and the doctor opened
the door. There was no point in refusing to get in. He
hadn't said a word, so she stayed silent too and sat
stiffly beside him and when they reached the apartment, got out quickly and went up to his front door,
relieved to find that Thompson, apparently possessed
of second sight, had already opened it.

'Five minutes, please, Thompson,' said the doctor
and swept Cordelia before him into his study, where
he dumped her gently into a chair and sat himself
behind his desk.

'Feeling better?' he wanted to know.

'I have never felt ill.' Her voice was cold.

'Ill? Who said you were ill? You shouldn't allow
your feelings to run away with you, you know.'

Her charming bosom swelled with indignation.
'My feelings are no concern of yours,' she told him
waspishly. 'Pray don't give them another thought.'

He smiled suddenly and she caught her breath. 'You don't like me,' he observed blandly, 'You think I'm a dull stick, buried in books and examination papers, living in a world of anaesthetic rooms and students and hospitals. It's true, I was hardly enthusiastic about you and Eileen coming here, I foresaw my peaceful studies being interrupted a dozen times a day. I find, to my surprise that I am left severely alone—sometimes—I have wondered if you were in the house, and strangely enough, I have lost my taste for study—I am no longer a bookworm. How do you account for that, Cordelia?'

She made herself forget the smile. 'Well,' she said seriously, 'I think perhaps...she was very beautiful, the lady who was here the other night. Eileen and I have thought that it would be very nice for you if you were to marry someone beautiful and stylish—like her.'

He was watching her gravely, his eyes alight with laughter. 'I'm touched that you—both of you—have my welfare to heart. That lady happens to be married.' He flicked a speck of dust off his sleeve. 'There are, of course, other ladies.'

A remark which depressed her. She said, 'Yes, of course. You don't mind that we—discussed you? Eileen is very fond of you...'

'I'm flattered. And you, Cordelia?'

She sat up straight. 'Me? I—you said I didn't like you?'

'In the heat of the moment,' he said gently, 'I can't be all that bad? Can I? Supposing I were to give up working on my book for a time and stuff my head with rather less medical matters, would you like me then, and not disappear every time I open a door, and I'll be firm about not reading my letters at breakfast?'

She studied his face. Quite serious, it was, although she couldn't see his eyes under the drooping lids. 'Oh, yes, I'm sure I'd like you, but that doesn't really matter does it?'

He stood up. 'I think perhaps it matters a good deal. Shall we have lunch?' He opened the door and as she went past him he asked casually: 'You're going back to the hospital later on, I expect? I sent some flowers and I wonder if you'd mind going along to the Graben or the Kohlmarkt and getting an armful of books?'

They sat down opposite each other and made polite conversation while she wondered what kind of a man he was. He had been warm and friendly in the study and now he was back in his reserved shell; polite and pleasant and obviously not minding if she were there at all. She remembered how he had kissed her and blushed at the thought, and blushed again when she looked up and found his eyes on her. She looked down at her plate as quickly as she could and missed his smile.

CHAPTER FIVE

EILEEN MADE good progress, but then, as her uncle pointed out, there was no reason why she shouldn't. The operation had been straightforward, the wound a mere couple of inches and the child in the best of health. She was out of bed by the end of the second day, already a little bored despite the frequent telephone conversations she held, regardless of expense, with her parents and Lady Trescombe. Her room resembled an expensive flower shop and as each visitor called to see her, they brought some trifle with them, so she was well on the way to becoming even more spoiled than ever. Cordelia, who had prided herself on instilling a little common humility into her, took things into her own hands after four days of Eileen's high flown tantrums. The child had been ill, but she had received every care and attention and now she was rapidly getting better. With luck she would be almost herself by the time her parents returned, which wouldn't be long now.

It had been a warm day and Eileen had been peevish and rude that morning; Cordelia, paying her usual evening visit took a quick, sympathetic look at her charge's cross face and said bracingly, 'Frau Keppel called this afternoon and asked when you would be starting your German lessons again.'

'But I'm only just recovering—I've been very ill.'

She burst into angry tears, 'I want to go back to Uncle's—he understands. You're hard hearted, Cordelia, I wish you'd go away and never come back.'

'I'll do that if you really want me to. Shall I tell you something, love? You are bored. I know it'll be a few weeks before you can do all the usual things but there are heaps of other things—like your German lessons—they'll pass an hour very nicely. Besides, Frau Keppel told me that she needs the money. Your uncle pays her handsomely but only when she gives you a lesson. She lives with her very old mother and two cats and they depend on her.'

Eileen had stopped crying. 'How do you know? Why should she tell you?'

'I expect I've got a listening kind of face.'

'I must agree with that,' said Dr Trescombe from behind her. 'Some people—women mostly, never listen, they either talk at the same time as I do or don't give me a chance to finish what I'm saying. Cordelia is polite enough to wait until I've finished however bored she may be.'

Eileen hunched a shoulder. 'Well, she hasn't got anything else to do now I'm ill and in pain.' She declared dramatically.

The doctor leaned his length over the end of the bed and stared down his handsome nose at it's occupant. 'Wrong. You are neither ill nor in pain so don't try and pull the wool over my eyes, I'm too old for it, and you're wrong about Cordelia. She writes a letter each day to your mother and another one to your grandmother, with a blow by blow account of your progress. And when she's not doing that, she's trotting to and fro to sit with you, and last but by no means least, she sorts my letters in the morning, guards my privacy when casual visitors call and answers the 'phone if Thompson isn't around.'

Which was all quite true, but he didn't mention that even when he was home they hardly met. Indeed breakfast was the only time she was sure of seeing him; she was beginning to get used to taking her meals in the little sitting room; either the doctor went out, very elegant in his dinner jacket, or shut himself in his study, presumably eating his dinner after she had gone to bed. He was polite, even vaguely friendly but there was no warmth in his manner. She didn't allow herself to think too much about that, aware that she would only make herself feel sad.

The doctor left presently and Eileen, presenting a sudden *volte-face*, conceded that German lessons weren't a bad idea and how about Cordelia bringing her needlework in the morning.'

Cordelia got up to go. 'Splendid—with luck you'll have it finished by the time your mother gets here and you'll be able to show off your German.' She submitted to Eileen's throttling embrace, and said, 'You'll grow into a nice person, Eileen—I shall dance at your wedding with real pleasure if you invite me, that is.'

'You'll get married first, darling Cordelia, and have lots of children and I'll have them for bride's attendants...'

Cordelia laughed. 'Go on with you! Remember to eat your supper and sleep well. I'll see you in the morning.'

She was half way down the long corridor leading to the entrance when she saw Dr Trescombe, students surging behind him, a stout middle-aged sister beside him, emerge from a door ahead of her. He was listening with bent head to what she was telling him and Cordelia slowed her pace, not wanting to be seen. She wished that she was clever; a ward sister who understood all the brilliant things he was doubtless discussing, making intelligent remarks to which he would listen, someone at whom he would actually look, someone he might even like... She stopped and let out a long sigh. Like wasn't what she meant; love was the word, she wanted him to love her more than anything in the world, just as she loved him. And why hadn't she discovered it sooner, this she was at a loss to understand. And why did she have to discover it now? Far better if she hadn't found out about it until she was safely back in England, miles away from him.

They had disappeared round a corner; she walked on again. Perhaps she was infatuated; after all, she had had precious little chance of meeting any young men during the last few years, perhaps it was the close proximity in which they lived... Not all that close, common sense told her and it wasn't infatuation, that wouldn't take into account his absent mindedness, his lack of enthusiasm at having her and Eileen in the apartment, his complete disregard of her, never more marked than these last few days when Eileen was in hospital. There was no point, she thought sadly, in buying any more new clothes, far better for her to save her money as a safeguard against an uncertain future.

She gained the outside and found him waiting for her and when she protested that the walk home would do her good, he merely opened the car's door and told her to get in. She did so meekly but the meekness was short lived.

'Why did you stop just now?' He wanted to know, 'as though you had discovered something momentous?'

'Me? But you didn't see—you were miles away—I...I don't know what you're talking about, I daresay I'd remembered something—forgotten something...' She stopped, suddenly aware that she was talking nonsense.

'Of course,' his voice was very smooth. 'How do you find Eileen?'

'Very well—bored stiff too.'

'I think we'd better have her back home in a couple of days time—her stitches will be out by then—that's if you could cope? She'll have to take things easily for a week or two, but there's no reason why she shouldn't go out each day for a short walk—supposing I hire a fiacre each day and you take a drive, and I must contrive to drive you out to the Vienna Woods before her parents get back.'

'Will she be able to go back to England when her parents come?' It was a relief to be able to talk about something which was impersonal.

'Heavens yes. They're going straight to Scotland and there's no question of school for her for the moment, anyway.'

'I see. She won't be going to see Lady Trescombe?'

He said carelessly, 'Oh as to that, I daresay they'll spend a day or two with her.' He stopped the car before the door. 'If you're not doing anything much this evening could you go through my post? Get it sorted out if you will and put it on my desk; I'm going out later on this evening and I'll go through it before I leave.' He leaned across and opened her door. 'You'll be going to see Eileen in the morning?'

She felt she should have added more than the bald 'Yes' she offered but he didn't seem to notice. 'I'm not coming in—I've an engagement, tell Thompson I'll be in to change later, will you?'

He nodded goodbye: 'I'll see you at breakfast.'

It was on the tip of her tongue to remark that he didn't see her at breakfast or anywhere else; she had become a useful appendage to his household, a nonentity to be forgotten the moment she left it. She ate her solitary dinner with no appetite, carefully having dealt with a large pile of letters, and then she went to bed.

In the morning after breakfast she took a tram to the shops to get some embroidery silks for Eileen, and then she went to be with her in the hospital. It was teatime when she got back, served in the small sitting room by Thompson, who murmured that Mrs Thompson had taken it upon herself to make a nice Madeira Cake and hoped that Miss Gibson would enjoy a slice.

For some reason Cordelia felt tearful at this kindly act; at least the Thompsons had never resented her.

There was no point in changing her dress; she did her face and hair and walked back to the hospital; at this hour of the late afternoon the trams were bulging with homegoers and the underground would be of no use to her. She found Eileen low spirited, but then she mostly was by the end of the day; however comfortably she was housed at the hospital, she felt shut in and was as well as that tired and peevish too.

Cordelia turned off the TV a ponderous speechmaker of no entertainment value, switched on some pleasant music on the radio and settled down to the task of cheering up her charge.

'How's the embroidery—there's not much more to do is there? You'll get it finished if you keep at it. Has your uncle been to see you?'

'I'm to come home in two days. Mummy 'phoned—they'll be here in ten days. Uncle Charles says I may go for rides each day...'

'Yes, he mentioned it.'

'And the Vienna Woods—he says he'll drive me there and have a picnic.'

So she wasn't to be included. How he must dislike her. 'You'll enjoy that.'

She hadn't meant to sound wistful but Eileen was a perceptive child. She asked, 'Do you miss me, Cordelia? Are you lonely?'

'Well, yes, of course I miss you—you're good company, love.'

She didn't see the sudden look of mischief on her companion's face. Eileen said sweetly: 'Well, I'll be back at Uncle Charles' house in a day or two, won't I. Cordelia, could you come a bit earlier tomorrow? About half-past nine?'

'Yes, of course, dear. Does that fit in better with the routine here?'

Eileen's smile was guileless. 'Yes, it does. You won't forget?' Eileen was still in bed when Cordelia arrived at the hospital the next morning; she wasn't alone, there was a young man with her, thick set, fair haired, blue eyed, a pleasant smile on his face.

Eileen's, 'Hullo, Cordelia, darling,' was splendidly casual, as was her equally casual introduction of the young man. 'This is Dr Julius Salfinger, Cordelia. He comes to see me most days when Uncle Charles is too busy. I call him Julius and I expect you can call him that too.'

She watched with a satisfied eye as they shook hands. 'Julius knows Vienna awfully well, he's lived here all his life. He says we ought to go to the Gala Rooms at the Hofburg Palace and see the imperial cutlery and silver and go to one of the real Viennese Restaurants for lunch.' She sighed deeply, 'but of course there won't be time now, will there? I mean I won't be well enough…'

'It seems a great shame,' observed Dr Salfinger, 'that you will have to miss these treats. But why cannot Cordelia…' He smiled at her, 'that is if she cares to—join me for lunch one day? You can be spared for that?'

'Uncle Charles told me that he was going to Salzburg this morning and wouldn't be back until this evening. Poor Cordelia will be all alone again.'

Cordelia hardly relished the forlorn picture her charge was painting of her. 'Oh, I've heaps to do,' she began.

'But you must stop for lunch? May I not call for you, Cordelia? I am free this afternoon and I would like very much to show you the silver when we have had lunch. Half-past twelve? At Dr Trescombe's apartment?'

It would have been churlish to refuse, besides, she didn't want to, it would fill an empty day with no hope of seeing Uncle Charles. She accepted nicely, mentally resolving to forget him and concentrate on Julius. She wasn't quite sure if she liked him, but it was hardly fair to form an opinion so quickly. Besides, it didn't really matter they were hardly likely to see each other again. The future suddenly loomed frighteningly close, and empty.

Julius was punctual, apparently delighted to be taking her out, but he was also, to her mind, too free with his compliments. She had no illusions about her looks and she thought he must either be blind or a terrible liar with his fulsome remarks. She did her best to ignore them, got into his Porsche and was whisked away to the side streets of Vienna where she had never quite dared to go and where, true to his word, Julius gave her lunch in a charming old-fashioned restaurant where he assured her the food was genuinely Viennese. He turned out to be a pleasant enough companion with a fund of light hearted stories about hospital life and a profound knowledge of the city. It was already two o'clock by the time they reached the Hofburg Palace and went to inspect the silver. This occupied them until three o'clock and since it was a splendid afternoon, Julius suggested that they might take a fiacre drive through the city. 'We can leave the car here and I'll drive you back after we've had tea somewhere.'

She refused pleasantly. 'I must get back—there are letters which must get the early evening post and somethings I must do for Eileen...'

She smiled at him. 'It's been a lovely afternoon and thank you very much—it was kind of you, you must have so many friends and family here in Vienna and not a great deal of free time.'

'Ah, but I have enjoyed it too, Cordelia. Please, we will do this again before you go back to England. Dinner one evening? Eileen will have to keep early hours for a few days and then you will be free, perhaps? I am sure that Dr Trescombe goes out a great deal in the evenings—he is a much sought after man, you know.' He shrugged his shoulders. 'But what would one expect? He is rich, handsome and clever— at the very peak of our profession. Although it must be admitted that he cares very little for our social life; he continues to study, he is writing a book and he travels frequently for he is much in demand. He will be missed.'

'He's going soon?' Cordelia was anxious to gather any crumb of information that she could.

'Within the next two or three weeks, I believe.' They were driving back to the apartment. 'Now about this dinner...'

She wished he wasn't so persistent. She had the feeling that he wasn't really keen to see her again and if that were true, why was he so anxious that she should accept his invitation. She said carefully: 'I

honestly can't be sure when I'm going to be free—
could we leave it for the moment?'

His heartiness was overpowering. 'Of course—I'll
see you at the hospital, but remember, I don't intend
to take no for an answer—there must be one evening
during the next week when you can be free. I shall
'phone you each day.'

He leaned across her and opened the door for her.
She got out and poked her head through the door once
more to thank him once again before he drove off.
When she turned round Dr Trescombe was on the
pavement behind her.

She was startled into saying stupidly, 'Oh, I
thought that you were in Salzburg…'

'When the cat's away?' He wanted to know in a
silky voice she didn't care for at all.

'Certainly not. I went to see Eileen this morning—
earlier than usual because she asked me to, Dr Salfinger was with her and—and he asked me to have lunch
with him and go to see the imperial cutlery. I have
lunched alone for days on end,' her voice rose
slightly, 'it was pleasant to have company.'

'Am I to stand corrected?' He wanted to know
blandly.

She flushed. 'No, of course not. I'm sorry if I
sounded rude, not,' she added matter-of-factly, 'that
I was any ruder than you were.'

He laughed then. 'Have you had tea? No? Then let
us go up to the apartment and share a soothing pot
between us.' As they went up to the flat, 'You like
young Salfinger?'

'It was very kind of him to ask me out to lunch,' she replied.

'I'm not surprised you aren't too keen,' said the doctor surprisingly. 'He's very much one for the girls.' He turned to look at her as he opened the apartment door. 'You're not at all his cup of tea,' he observed coolly.

Cordelia stared up at him, her face very red. She said, her teeth chattering with rage. 'I am paid to look after Eileen,' she told him in a voice she strove to keep steady, 'not to be the butt of your rudeness, Dr Trescombe.'

She ducked past him and skimmed along the hall and up the steps, bent on reaching her room and staying there. He overtook her quite easily before she could get her hand on the doorknob. His large, firm hand closed over hers, gently prising it off, not letting go.

'Blame my lack of female company—I have become uncouth. I said it all wrong, didn't I?'

She tugged at her hand with no success at all, and muttered darkly, not looking at him.

'Cordelia, be good enough to look at me.' And when she didn't, he put his free hand under her chin so that she had to meet his eyes. He went on deliberately, 'You're not his cup of tea; not his sort—you don't know much about men, do you? He's out for a good time and you're easy game—a few days of what he calls fun and you'll be gone and he'll forget you.' He added, 'I'd prefer you not to see him again, Cordelia.'

Her tongue betrayed her thoughts before she could curb it. 'Why do you bother?'

His face became as austere as his voice had been. 'I am responsible for your welfare while you are under my roof.' He let her hand go at last and Thompson who had come into the hall to enquire about tea, had trotted away again to tell Mrs Cook all about it and then gone back into the hall, making sure that they heard him this time.

When she joined him presently she had expected to feel awkward but Dr Salfinger wasn't mentioned, indeed, Dr Trescombe behaved as though they had just that moment met. She never would understand him, she thought despondently, even though she loved him so. She answered his polite impersonal remarks in like fashion and was glad when she could escape to her room. Quite easy as it happened, for he observed as he put down his cup and saucer that he had some reading to do.

But he came out of his study ten minutes later and left the house, driving away in the Jaguar, and Cordelia, washing her hair, never heard him go, nor did a strangely subdued Eileen, when she visited her later on that evening, think fit to tell her of her uncle's visit. Uncle Charles had asked a number of pertinent questions he had had no difficulty in worming her rather silly little plot from her.

'Why did you do it, Eileen?' He had asked her, 'had you thought that you might hurt Cordelia?'

She had protested against that. 'I wanted her to have some fun—she was lonely, Uncle Charles, she never goes anywhere, only with me when I'm there, and once to a concert with you. I thought she might like a boyfriend.'

'Your intentions may have been good my dear, but young Dr Salfinger is hardly...why him?'

'I told him about Cordelia and he thought it would be fun to take her out and pretend that he'd fallen for her.' Said Eileen sulkily. 'So I got her to come early so that he could meet her here.'

He looked at her in silence and she said: 'Are you angry Uncle Charles?'

'Yes, I am. You see, Eileen, Cordelia is a nice girl; not the kind of person people play tricks on. I daresay she thought that young Salfinger really wanted to take her out and if she discovered the truth she'd be upset.' He smiled suddenly: 'Don't play Cupid again, my dear; leave Cordelia to find her own love.'

'But she never will, she never meets any one, only Thompson and Mrs Thompson and me—and you of course.'

Her uncle went to look out of the window. 'Ah, but there's magic in Vienna, didn't you know? Anything might happen. Shall we wait and see?' He walked over to her and kissed her swiftly. 'Not a word, Eileen, cross your heart?'

'Cross my heart. How long must we wait for something magic to happen?'

'Not too long, my dear.' He glanced at his watch. 'I must go—I'm late.'

And Cordelia, having no inkling of this conversation, was delighted to find her charge so anxious to agree to her plans for the resuming of drawing lessons as soon as she got back to her uncle's. She walked

back to the apartment presently, her head full of
schemes for keeping Eileen happy for the last week
before her parents arrived. It wasn't until she was
getting ready for bed after her solitary dinner, that she
spared a thought for Julius Salfinger. Dr Trescombe
had been very definite about her not seeing him again
and it might be difficult putting him off. She would
have to think of some watertight excuse if he 'phoned.
She didn't think about him for long; she curled up in
bed and allowed herself at last the pleasure of thinking about Charles Trescombe. Of course, it was a singularly profitless exercise; in a little more than a week
he would wish her a pleasant goodbye and that would
be that. She wouldn't see him again after that, even
though he was going back to England she saw no
chance of their paths crossing; she really would have
to think seriously about another job. Instead, she went
over the conversation they had had that afternoon,
word for word, and not just once.

Julius Salfinger 'phoned the next day, but she was
out and Thompson, offering to take a message had
been told not to bother. Cordelia heaved a sigh of
relief when she was told; Eileen would be coming
home late the following afternoon and once she was
back, she could give the perfectly true excuse that she
must stay with her until her parents returned. But she
had reckoned without Fate. She had brought back a
good many of the odds and ends Eileen had collected
while she was in hospital on the previous evening and
she wasn't going again until tea time, when Eileen's
uncle would bring the child home, and she would
pack up the rest of Eileen's things at the same time.

That left her with a morning to herself and since time was running out, she decided to walk through some of the older streets of Vienna and treat herself to coffee at Sacher's. It was a brilliant morning; the doctor had left the apartment directly after breakfast with a brief reminder that she should be at the hospital by four o'clock to help Eileen collect her things ready for him to pick them up shortly after. 'If there are any messages for me at lunchtime, 'phone me at the hospital, will you?' he had asked as he went, so that her vague idea about staying out to lunch was squashed. All the same, she had several hours of the morning to herself, she took a tram to Heldenplatz and started walking in the direction of St Stephan's Cathedral, taking any small street she fancied, keeping it's tall spire in view.

Her way took her close to Graben, so that she lingered to look in the shops there. She was admiring the beautifully arranged flowers in a florist's window when someone took her arm.

Julius Salfinger—the last person she wanted to see.

'What luck,' he began, 'and how pretty you look this morning. What about that dinner date? I know of an enchanting little restaurant!'

She said pleasantly, 'Hullo Julius. I'm afraid I won't be able to have dinner with you—Eileen's coming home today—you know that, of course—and I'll not be free now until her parent's arrive.'

'Nonsense—of course you can manage an evening. When the child's in bed she'll come to no harm—you can slip out, no one need know...'

'I couldn't do that, I'm sorry, Julius.'

His smile faded. 'Standing me up, my dear? I don't imagine that you get many dates, do you? I would never have asked you out in the first place if it hadn't been for young Eileen trading on my good nature with her tale of a poor young woman with no money and no chance of having a bit of fun. I'm sorry I put myself out.'

Cordelia felt rage and humiliation rising in her throat, choking her. She said in a voice which didn't sound like her own any more. 'Then why did you ask me out to dinner? Surely giving me lunch was all that your—your pity demanded?'

He said sulkily. 'Girls enjoy my company, they can't wait to be asked out again...'

'Well, here is one who doesn't; you're conceited...' She swallowed the tirade on her tongue and marched past him into the nearest shop. It was a superior gentlemen's outfitters and the sauve young man who came to see what she wanted was quite put out when she refused to look at Italian silk ties and dressy waistcoats, indeed, after a few perplexed minutes he came to the conclusion that she hadn't heard him or even seen him. She hadn't—she was unaware of her surroundings, wrapped in such bitter thoughts that she felt sick.

She left the shop presently, walking quickly, not caring where she was going, presently she found herself by the Cathedral but she didn't go inside turning away and going towards the Parkring and crossing it to go into the Stadtpark, where she walked the paths until she was quite tired when she stopped at a small café and had coffee. She glanced at her watch and knew that she would have to get a tram back to the apartment. She had no wish to return but Dr Trescombe had asked her to let him know if there were any messages. Sitting in the tram she tried to think sensibly. Should she confront Eileen with the whole sorry little episode or pretend that she knew nothing about it? And what about the doctor? She had an uneasy feeling that he might conceivably have had something to say to his niece who would probably pour the whole story out. She closed her eyes at the awful thought; he didn't think much of her and now he would add impatient pity for the rather dull girl with no looks to speak of. She looked out of the window, her eyes wide to stop the tears falling.

She pecked at the delicious lunch Mrs Thompson had got for her, watched by a solicitous Thompson and since there were no messages to pass on to the hospital she took herself off to her room where she had a good cry, washed her face with cold water, made it up with extra care under the impression that she had disguised the tears successfully and went to the hospital, and as ill-luck would have it, the first person she saw there was Dr Trescombe, standing by the reception desk, talking to Julius Salfinger. She stopped short but only for a moment and then went past them with a murmured good afternoon, aware that her face was as red as a beet. An occasion, she thought, wryly, when it would have been nice if the ground could have opened beneath her and she could have disappeared from sight; preferably to come up again somewhere a long way away—England, perhaps.

Of course she didn't see the embarrassment on Dr
Salfinger's face nor the thoughtful glance Dr Trescombe gave to each one of them. The thoughtfulness
was replaced by a bland expression which seemed to
upset the younger man, for he nipped away smartly
when Dr Trescombe dismissed him, still blandly but
with a nasty steely look in his eyes.

Cordelia took a deep breath outside Eileen's door
before she went in; it wasn't any good being cross
with the child, she had every intention of saying nothing at all and as it happened it was easier than she
had imagined. She bustled around, finishing the last
of the packing, hardly noticing that Eileen was rather
silent. She had her head in the locker by the bed,
making sure it was empty when the doctor came in
and she lingered for a moment, bracing herself for
whatever he might say.

But beyond a pleasant remark about everyone being fortunate to meet at the time he had suggested, he
said nothing at all and presently sent Eileen along the
corridor to Sister's office to bid that lady goodbye.
Which left Cordelia standing with nothing to do,
wishing herself anywhere but where she was, for he
was leaning against the wall staring at her.

After a moment, he said: 'You've been crying...'

She took a quick look at him; there was neither
curiosity nor pity in his face, merely an impersonal
kindness which strangely enough made her want to
burst into tears again. 'Well, you know, don't you? I
can see that you do—I feel so—so humiliated. But
you are not to be angry with Eileen; Dr Salfinger—I
met him this morning—accidentally—he told me...

She wanted me to have some fun—she's only a child.' She ended her voice suddenly gruff with anger. 'You're not to say a word.'

He eased his shoulders against the wall and put his hands in his pockets.

'But I already have—yesterday. You see, I guessed a good deal of all this when you told me you'd been out with young Salfinger—I did tell you that you weren't his cup of tea, and that set me thinking. Eileen told me everything when I came to see her.'

Cordelia said fiercely: 'There's no need for all this meddling. I'm quite able to look after myself.' She added with a fine lack of logic, 'Only I thought that perhaps he'd really meant it—I mean wanting to take me out.' She lifted her chin. 'There's no harm done, and as I said, there's been enough meddling.'

'I stand corrected, Cordelia. If you're quite sure everything is packed, shall we go? I believe Mrs Thompson has laid on a splendid tea for Eileen.'

She had deserved the snub. She said that yes, she was quite ready and when Eileen came back, plunged on into plans for that young lady's amusement during the next few days. This kept the conversational ball rolling until they got to the apartment, when there was a prolonged welcome from the Thompsons before they ate the splendid tea Mrs Thompson had ready for them, during which meal, Cordelia, the bit between the teeth, sustained a cheerful discussion as to which day would be best for Eileen to go to the Vienna Woods. They hadn't made a decision when the doctor got up, observing that he had some work to do in his study and that Eileen was to go to bed within the next hour. 'And no arguing, my dear—if you're not one hundred per cent fit when your mother arrives, I'll never live it down. You can have your supper in bed; Mrs Thompson has her head crammed with all the delicious tempting dishes she intends to offer you.' He paused at the door. 'Cordelia, I'd like to see you later, I have to go out this evening, perhaps when you have seen Eileen safely into her bed and before you have dinner? Come to the study.'

When he had gone Eileen turned a scared face towards Cordelia.

'He's not going to send you away?' She gulped. 'It's all my—Uncle Charles said I wasn't to tell you, but I must…'

Cordelia smiled very kindly. 'It's all right love, I know all about it. I'm not cross, really I'm not, I think it was rather sweet of you to bother about me. We'll not say any more about it. After all I had a lovely lunch.' She managed a cheerful grin and Eileen grinned back.

'You're really a darling,' she declared. 'It's such a relief.' She frowned, 'why do you suppose Uncle Charles wants to see you?'

'I daresay he's going to let me know what is to happen when your parents get here,' said Cordelia calmly. 'I expect I'll travel back with you but it'll be for your mother and father to decide what's to happen after that.'

'I want you to stay,' said Eileen stormily. 'I've been ill, I mustn't be thwarted.'

'But you'll be well again by then,' observed Cordelia reasonably, 'ready for school after a holiday in

Scotland. Anyway let's wait and see, shall we? Now what about your supper? What do you fancy?'

Eileen wasn't to be hurried she changed her mind several times and by then Cordelia considered that it was high time that she went to her bed. Eileen wasn't to be hurried over that either, but finally she was settled with a tray of delicacies on the bed table and Cordelia went to her room to tidy herself. She was going to be alone again; there was no need to change her dress, she brushed her hair severely, did her face, and feeling sick with apprehension and at the same time excited because she would be with Charles Trescombe, even if only for a few minutes, she went downstairs. The apartment was quiet; Mrs Thompson would be putting the final touches to her dinner, the doctor, presumably, was buried in his books in the study. She knocked on the door and at his quiet 'Come in', opened the door.

CHAPTER SIX

THE DOCTOR WAS sitting at his desk amidst a welter of opened tomes and closely written sheets. He got up and pulled a chair forward and waved Cordelia into it, sat down again and said nothing. Cordelia waited for a minute or so and then said mildly, 'You wanted to see me, Dr Trescombe.'

'Yes—yes, I did. You are prepared to go back with Eileen and her parents when they come? I'm afraid I have no idea what arrangements they will choose to make with you, it seems to me very likely that they will ask you to stay on with them for a time. You are ready to do that?'

'Oh, yes, if they would like me to.'

He was staring at her and she found it hard to look away.

He said slowly: 'You have been of very great benefit to Eileen—she's a dear child, but spoilt; used to having her own way and creating havoc if she can't get it, and you have checked that to a large extent. I—I and I'm sure her mother and father too—are most grateful for that.'

'Thank you,' said Cordelia politely, and waited; he surely hadn't wanted to see her just to say that.

'I have arranged to be free on Saturday. We might drive to the Vienna Woods and perhaps have lunch at one of the little restaurants there. I should be obliged if you will come too, Cordelia—we will leave mid morning and return directly after tea, that will be a long enough day for Eileen, besides I have a dinner engagement.'

'Very well, Doctor. Eileen will enjoy that.' She could hear her voice, very stiff and she tried to remedy matters. 'I shall enjoy it too. Is there anything else?'

The doctor sighed and shook his head. 'No, I think not. You have been happy here? Cordelia?'

'Me? Oh, yes thank you. Vienna's a lovely city, isn't it? And we've seen quite a lot of it...'

'But you?' He persisted, 'you haven't felt homesick or lonely?'

She thought of her bleak life with her stepmother and the children. 'No, neither.'

'I suppose that is fortunate, since this is your work and it may carry you a long way from home.'

She wondered what he would say if she told him that she had no home any more. It was surprising that two people could live in the same house for weeks on end and know nothing about each other. And still more surprising that she could love him so whole heartedly and yet know so little of him.

She remembered that he was going out that evening and got up. 'I'll say good night, Doctor.'

He got up and opened the door. 'Good night, Cordelia.' She had the impression that he was going to say something else, but he didn't and she went to the little sitting-room where Thompson had laid the table for her dinner.

The next few days were uneventful; Eileen, with

the prospect of her parents arriving within the week, gave up her role of interesting invalid and became so active that Cordelia had to restrain her from doing too much. The daily rides in the fiacre helped, of course, she took care to choose somewhere interesting to visit and since the weather stayed fine the afternoons at least were taken care of. German lessons took up the mornings and the evenings were spent playing Scrabble or cards. Of the doctor they saw very little; he joined them for meals and once, while they were out driving, he swept past them in his car, a striking looking woman sitting beside him. Cordelia spent the rest of the day wondering who she was, unable to accept Eileen's instant guess that she was one of Uncle Charles's girl friends. She was none the wiser when the doctor mentioned at dinner that evening that he had seen them that afternoon for although Eileen said instantly: 'You had a lady with you, Uncle Charles,' he dismissed the remark with a casual, 'So I did,' and rather pointedly asked how the German lessons were going.

To Cordelia he was polite and beyond wanting to know how Eileen fared showed no interest in her day. But then, she told herself sensibly, why should he?'

Saturday came, a splendid morning with the promise of a hot day. There was a delay while Eileen made up her mind what she should wear and then changed it again but her uncle bore this with commendable patience and presently settled them in the car; his niece beside him and Cordelia, neat and cool in a cotton skirt and top, in the back.

He took them through the wine growing villages of

Grinzing, Sievering and Nüssdorf, up the slopes of the Wienerwald, slowing so that they might look around them, and then driving on, taking the shady lanes between the trees. Cordelia lost all sense of direction presently; not that it mattered, she was perfectly content to gaze around her and join in Eileen's enthusiasm for the picturesque inns they passed and got out very readily when the doctor stopped before one of these and suggested coffee. They sat on a balcony with trees all around them and the doctor laid himself out to be a charming companion—quite different to his usual self, she decided. Perhaps it was the sports shirt and slacks, so different too from his sober grey suits, but he seemed another man entirely. Perhaps because he knew that very soon now she and Eileen would be gone and he would be shot of the pair of them. He would go back to his dry-as-dust work, interlarded with dinners with lovely girls like the one she had seen. Jealousy, something she had never experienced before, very nearly curdled the cream in her coffee.

She realised that the doctor was addressing her and saw that he was smiling faintly. 'So sorry,' she was annoyed to feel her cheeks grow pink, 'I was thinking…'

'I was asking you if you liked it here sufficiently to return?'

She said promptly. 'You mean if I should be offered a job here at some time? Oh, yes, I'd come—it's beautiful, and it must take some months to see everything.' She looked around her. 'It's beautiful here and there must be lots more to it than *Tales from the Vienna Woods*!'

'There is. Did you know that this is a great wine-growing district? And each year when the wine is ready, people stream here to sample it. They drink it in places called Heurigen and they know where to go because there is a pine pole hung above the door.' He paused: 'I'm not boring you?'

'No, oh, no. I've been longing to ask questions…'

He raised his eyebrows. 'Am I such an ogre, Cordelia?'

'No, of course not, Doctor, only—well, you have your work and your interests.'

'So I have. I begin to think that they are not enough.' He sat back in his chair and glanced at Eileen who had wandered off to play with the restaurant puppy. 'Well, it seems a good enough time to ask more questions, doesn't it?'

'Just a few—the Prater—we've not been there, because I'm not exactly sure what it is—an amusement park? And is it suitable for Eileen?'

'Not until she's quite her old self. It's a hive of activities—sports, fair ground, a trade fair, swimming pool, race course—the lot. But somehow I don't think it's quite your taste, Cordelia. A visit to look round, perhaps—you should have a country garden for a background…'

This was so unexpected that she stayed silent.

'Liberty prints and your hair hanging down your back.' But she must have dreamt that bit for he went on in a very ordinary voice: 'I doubt if you've been to mass in the Hofburg Chapel although you'll know

NO POSTAGE
NECESSARY
IF MAILED
IN THE
UNITED STATES

BUSINESS REPLY MAIL
FIRST-CLASS MAIL   PERMIT NO. 717   BUFFALO, NY

POSTAGE WILL BE PAID BY ADDRESSEE

HARLEQUIN READER SERVICE
3010 WALDEN AVE
PO BOX 1867
BUFFALO NY 14240-9952

GET FREE BOOKS
and a
FREE GIFT WHEN YOU PLAY THE...

LAS VEGAS
GAME

Just scratch off the gold box with a coin. Then check below to see the gifts you get!

YES!

I have scratched off the gold Box. Please send me my **2 FREE BOOKS** and gift for which I qualify. I understand that I am under no obligation to purchase any books as explained on the back of this card.

386 HDL DCNG

186 HDL DCM5
(H-RB-0S-02/01)

NAME (PLEASE PRINT CLEARLY)

ADDRESS

APT.#   CITY

STATE/PROV.   ZIP/POSTAL CODE

7	**7**	**7**

Worth TWO FREE BOOKS plus a BONUS Mystery Gift!

Worth TWO FREE BOOKS!

TRY AGAIN!

Offer limited to one per household and not valid to current Harlequin Romance® subscribers. All orders subject to approval.

all about the Vienna Boy's Choir—only for subscribers though—and tucked away in a corner of the Hofburg Palace there are work rooms where the tapestries and carpets are repaired and mended. Indeed, it's difficult to know where to go first, it's such a rambling place. What did you see with young Salfinger?'

'The silver...'

'That was all? A pity that you are returning to England in a few days time, and there's a great deal still for you to see here.'

'Yes, I know. But I'm glad that I've seen so much—I'll always remember it...' and you, she added silently.

Eileen came wandering back then and they got into the car once more and drove on. 'We're going to Klosterneuburg,' observed the doctor—'I thought we'd make a rough circle round Vienna, and that's a good spot for a picnic.'

The picnic was a great success; Mrs Thompson had packed a basket with the kind of food one read about in glossy magazines and when they had eaten almost all of it, they stretched out under the trees talking. Cordelia couldn't remember any of their conversation afterwards, only that they had all had a share in it and had laughed a great deal.

They drove slowly back to Vienna taking a roundabout route and stopping for tea and gigantic cream cakes on the way. It was a delightful place but Cordelia was glad that the doctor had decided to take a picnic instead of lunching at a restaurant, she was going to remember the day for always; it would be a cherished memory.

Eileen was tired when they got back. 'Bed,' said Cordelia firmly, 'you can have your supper on a tray,' and when the child would have argued: 'No, love, you're tired. You've had a lovely day, and I daresay we'll think of something interesting to do tomorrow.'

Eileen after a token and half hearted denial of tiredness, followed her to her room willingly enough. Cordelia added her own good night to her charge as the doctor, with the briefest of nods, crossed the hall to his study. Half an hour with his face in a book, thought Cordelia, before he had that dinner date. She saw Eileen into bed, tidied the bathroom, sat for ten minutes on the end of the bed, making suggestions for the next day and went down to see what Mrs Thompson could produce for supper.

Cold watercress soup, suggested that admirable lady, chicken vol-au-vents, creamed potatoes and aubergines cooked in butter and a sorbet for afters.

'It sounds delicious', declared Cordelia, 'and I'll have mine on a tray, Mrs Thompson—you've got the extra bother of sending up Eileen's supper, and I'll be on my own...'

She hadn't heard the door open behind her. 'No, you'll be with me,' observed the doctor blandly, 'you really can't leave Vienna without seeing the Prater Park—there's a good restaurant there, and if you feel you must be cultural, I'll take you to Praterstrasse and you can take a look at the house where Strauss composed the Blue Danube.'

Cordelia stared up at him. 'But you have a dinner engagement—you said so'.

'I cried off.' And at her astonished look: 'Don't

look like that—I shan't be missed. Besides I have a great wish to see the Prater Park too.'

Cordelia said a little wildly: 'Oh, have you. But Eileen—she's in bed.'

'The right place for her; she's had a long day. Mrs Thompson will keep a motherly eye on her, won't you, Mrs Thompson?'

'Of course, Sir. She'll be no trouble. If I take her supper up in half an hour?'

'And in the meantime you can get yourself ready, Cordelia. Bring a wrap of some sort—it'll be chilly later on. Will an hour suit you?'

She nodded and added childishly, 'What shall I wear?'

His face was very kind. 'A summer dress—that pale silky thing you wear will do nicely.'

She showered and did her face and hair and got into the silk jersey dress and went to see how Eileen was getting on. Enjoying a hearty supper, by the look of it with the radio belting out pop music and a book propped up on the tray.

'You look nice,' she observed with her mouth full. 'I can't think what's come over Uncle Charles—perhaps it's a kind of a farewell treat—after all he hasn't entertained you at all, has he?'

'Well, he had no need to,' said Cordelia reasonably, 'I'm your governess, my dear, not his guest.'

'Well, I hope you can think of something to talk about. There's one thing, he never bores on about being a doctor, does he? He'd be quite nice if he got married and had a woman's softening influence…

Cordelia giggled. 'You are the most ridiculous

child.' She dropped a kiss on Eileen's cheek. 'I shan't tell you to be good—you're too old for that, but please put out the light at nine o'clock and go to sleep.'

'OK, but if I wake up when you come back you're to tell me about it.' She inspected the sorbet and picked up a spoon. 'You know—what kind of an evening you've had. Uncle Charles might find you quite fun.'

Cordelia doubted that.

He was waiting for her in the hall, sitting on the wall table, reading. He got up when he saw her and put the book down and she thought how very good looking he was. He wasn't wearing his usual sober grey suit either, but a blazer and a tie which she was sure signified some club or old school or the like. His pale fawn slacks were faultlessly cut and he looked at least ten years younger. She loved him to distraction and the contrast between them, in her opinion was cruel.

'Eileen all right?' He asked easily.

'Oh, yes. Eating a huge supper with the radio blaring…she's promised to put out her light at nine o'clock. She's tired but she loved her day.'

'And you? Did you love your day too?'

'Yes, oh yes, very much thank you.'

'Good. Let us hope that you will find this evening just as enjoyable.'

She did, of course. She would have been happy digging potatoes or sweeping streets with Charles, as it was she was ecstatic; the one fly in her ointment was the doubt that she was being as entertaining as he would like. She had had little chance of practising amusing conversation during the last few years, besides she was a little shy of him. It didn't enter her head that he might enjoy a companion who listened when he talked, refrained from making catty comments about the people around them, and maintained a restful silence without apparently feeling that she should fill it with mindless chatter.

They dined in a former Emperor's hunting lodge—a meal worthy of it's surroundings; lobster patties, and then a Hungarian dish; smoked duck with stuffed cabbage and to finish a magnificent confection of fruit, chocolate, nuts, ice cream and whipped cream. To accompany these the doctor ordered *Durnsteiner Katzensprung*: a wine from Durnstein, a picturesque village on the other bank of the Danube, and when Cordelia asked him to translate its name he told her 'Cats Leap', the kindly cat face on the label implying that it carried no hangover with it. 'So we can safely drink the bottle between us,' he assured her and smiled at her with such charm that her heart knocked against her ribs.

By the time they had had coffee the long summer evening was sliding slowly into dusk. There were lights everywhere now, and crowds of people intent on enjoying themselves. 'The fun fair, I think,' suggested the doctor and took her arm.

Cordelia, not having had much fun for several years, was entranced; egged on by her companion, she had a go at everything; aiming at coconuts with the earnestness of a child, having her fortune told, watching the sword swallower; trying her skill at the shoot-

ing gallery because she wanted the prize—a small
teddy bear. She had no luck but the doctor did and
she tucked the furry toy under one arm and when
invited, had a session on the dodgems. It was rather
a tight squeeze, the pair of them in the little car and
it made more room when the doctor put his arm
around her. The giant Ferris wheel she refused to try
and he didn't attempt to persuade her, suggesting instead that they might walk through the park and find
somewhere they could have some more coffee. Sitting
opposite him presently, while the waiter took their
order, she tried to thank him for her lovely evening
but he waved her thanks aside. 'You certainly deserve
an evening out,' he told her carelessly, 'the least I
could do for you after the time you've had with Eileen. When you came you assured me that neither of
you would trouble me in any way, and you haven't.
Indeed, I was scarcely aware of you in the apartment.'

Just the sort of speech to take all the shine out of
her evening. And there was no way in which to answer it. She smiled vaguely in his direction suddenly
self conscious, aware that he expected her to say
something.

'You'll be glad to have the apartment to yourself,
I expect,' she observed in an over bright voice.

'I'm leaving Vienna very shortly. I shall go back
to my practice.'

He was leaning back in his chair smiling faintly,
watching her and she sought feverishly for something
to say, 'Your book? Thompson told me that you were
writing one—is it finished?'

'Yes. What are your plans for tomorrow?'

A snub—presumably he could ask questions of her, but she might not of him. It made her aware of her position in the household so that she answered stiffly: 'When we went to Schonbrunn I promised that I would take Eileen back before we left Vienna, we didn't have time to see everything.' She added, 'So I thought we might go there tomorrow; we could take a taxi or a fiacre and I'll not let her do too much.'

'We'll go in the car—an early lunch I think and we can have tea somewhere. Did you see the coach museum?' And when she shook her head, 'we can walk down the linden tree avenue—I imagine the Gloriette will be too far for Eileen—if you feel like it though, I'll stay with her while you walk to the top and take a closer look.'

'Am I to come with you?'

He didn't answer at once and she thought that perhaps he hadn't heard her. 'Oh, yes Cordelia, you have become very necessary—in fact indispensable. Your family must miss you very much.'

A difficult remark to answer. 'Well, my stepbrothers and sisters are a good deal younger than I...'

'Yes, of course—I should have told you weeks ago to 'phone to your home whenever you wished, but I daresay you write to each other.'

She peeped quickly at him but his face was as placid as his voice had been; just for a moment she had the feeling that he was probing. She remembered uneasily that all the post was put by his plate on the breakfast table each morning and the afternoon letters were left on the hall table for everyone to see. If he had bothered to look, he would have noticed that she never had any letters. She said 'of course', in a voice which unused to lying, betrayed itself.

It was a relief when he began to talk about something quite different and presently suggested that they might continue their stroll through the park. Cordelia, glancing at her watch and seeing how late it was, hesitated. 'It's half-past eleven…' She pointed out.

'You'd like to go back home? We can walk this way—the car's only five minutes away.' His tone was easy and made her feel quite put out.

She was still more put out when they arrived back at the apartment and after bidding her a polite good night, he glanced at his watch and let himself out again. Cordelia stood in the hall, not sure whether to laugh or cry. She had had no time to thank him for her evening, indeed, she had the impression that he couldn't get away fast enough. What should have been an evening to remember had turned sour. She went on standing there, staring aimlessly at the door, disappointment welling up inside her. She would not go to Schonbrunn she decided then and there; she would have a headache or a sore throat then the doctor could exert himself to entertain his niece. Thank heaven Eileen's parents would soon be back and she could go away from this hateful place and never see him again… At this point the door opened and the doctor walked in again. She saw that there was a certain urgency in his manner as he crossed the hall, caught her hand and urged her back towards the door. 'There's been an accident,' he told her. 'You can help.' He raised his voice shouting for Thompson and when he came hurrying, told him to 'phone the police and send them to the house next door. Thompson was far too good a servant to waste time asking questions, he said 'Yes, Sir,' in an unhurried manner and went to the 'phone.

The doctor drew Cordelia outside into the corridor and hurried her down the stairs and into the street. The apartment house next door was exactly the same as the one they had left, its wide porch shrouded in shadow.

The doctor then opened his car door and took out a powerful torch and handed it to Cordelia, took his bag from the back and said tersely. 'In the porch, shine the torch when I say so. I hope you're not squeamish.'

She hoped she wasn't too, but she did as he told her and gave an involuntary gasp as the powerful beam lighted up the inert figure sprawling by the door. There was a lot of blood and the figure was very still. She held the torch with both hands to keep it steady and asked in a dry whisper, 'Is he dead?'

'No, hold that torch still, I must stop this bleeding.'

He was undoing the man's jacket and pulling up the stained shirt and Cordelia prudently shut her eyes. She was a sensible girl, but the man looked ghastly and she was feeling a little sick. All the same, after a moment she opened them cautiously to see what the doctor was doing. He had exposed the wound; no, several wounds, she saw, quite small stab wounds in the man's chest, surely not large enough to make such a fearful mess...

'Bring that torch nearer,' commanded the doctor, and she did so, her teeth clenched, and noticed that the hem of her dress was spattered with blood. Hardly the time to worry about such things, she told herself, with the poor man lying there, desperately ill, but all the same the dress was probably ruined. She took another look at the man and swallowed hard; she mustn't be sick at all costs.

'A little nearer,' said the doctor, intent on what he was doing. 'The police ambulance should be here by now, and the police.'

Obedient to their cue, they arrived together seconds later, armed, thank heaven with their own torches, so that Cordelia was able to switch off hers and put it back in the car, and then, because everyone was intent on the man lying there, slipping back next door, up the stairs and thankfully into the doctor's apartment, where Thompson was waiting. He took one look at her white face, sat her down and fetched her a glass of brandy.

'Ugh, I hate the stuff,' said Cordelia and obediently swallowed. It made her feel better though, and she was able to tell Thompson what had happened. 'Though I've no idea what happened or who the man is,' she finished.

'No doubt the doctor will find out, Miss,' said Thompson soothingly. 'He'll go to the hospital and hand him over, I daresay.' He studied her in a fatherly fashion: 'A nice pot of tea, Miss—I'll get Mrs Thompson to make it at once. You go into the drawing room and I'll bring it.'

She drank two cups, decided against a third and prepared to go up to bed; the doctor might be away for hours yet, and even if he wasn't he wouldn't want to find her still sitting up. But the chair was comfortable and she was suddenly sleepy. Five minutes, she promised herself and closed her eyes. When she opened them he was sitting opposite to her, well back in his chair, a glass of whisky in his hand, reading.

'Ah—oh,' said Cordelia wildly, 'I went to sleep— I'm sorry, I didn't...'

He closed the book and put it on the table beside him. 'Don't apologise, you look quite charming when you're sleeping.'

Did he mean that she looked the reverse when she was awake? She didn't dare ask.

'Oh,' she said, 'well, I'll go to bed...'

'Don't you want to know what has happened to the man?'

'Yes, of course I do, but I don't expect you want to talk now.'

'Then you suppose wrong. I have always envied my married friends who go home at ungodly hours and find their wives waiting with hot drinks and a ready ear.'

He must be joking. She said coldly: 'I have no doubt that you could remedy that if you should wish to, Doctor.'

He smiled. 'Of course. Indeed, I intend to do so very shortly.' He added kindly just in case she hadn't understood. 'Get married, you know.'

She said bleakly: 'How nice. I hope you'll be very happy.'

'I have no doubt of that. Would you like a drink? No? You behaved with commendable aplomb this evening—I'm sorry that your evening was spoiled,

Cordelia. The man will recover; he'd lost a lot of blood but as far as could be seen at the preliminary examination, nothing vital had been hurt.'

'I'm glad. Does anyone know who he is?'

'No idea at the moment, the police will get on to that. He'll be well looked after.' He put down his glass. 'What about tomorrow? Lunch at noon I think, that will give us a long afternoon. But take a look at Eileen before you say anything, will you? She's pretty fit now, but she mustn't get overtired.' He got to his feet. 'And bed for you too.'

He went and opened the door for her and as she went past him, put out a hand and caught her gently by the arm. 'Good night, Cordelia,' his voice was gentle...so was the kiss he gave her.

'Oh,' said Cordelia for the third time and scooted across the hall and up the steps and along the corridor to her room, she heard the doctor laughing softly as she closed the door, and what with that and tiredness and a delayed fright at the evenings happenings, she began to cry. She cried steadily while she undressed, showered and went to peep at Eileen. She was still weeping when she fell asleep.

The remembrance of her tears annoyed her very much when she woke up in the morning. As a consequence she was very brisk and cheerful when she went to see how Eileen fared. That young lady took one look at her and wanted to know why she had been crying, which, considering Cordelia had taken a good deal of time in making up her face, was vexing.

She decided to ignore the question and embarked instead on a breezy account of the Prater Park which lasted nicely until the pair of them went downstairs for breakfast.

It being Sunday, there was no post, which meant that the doctor was able to devote all his attention to them. He wished them good morning, hoped that they had slept well, and recommended the scrambled eggs.

'Cordelia's been crying,' said Eileen in a clear voice not to be ignored.

The doctor shot a quick glance at Cordelia, busy with the coffee pot and pink in the face, moreover he saw that her hands were shaking. Possibly with rage, he thought with secret amusement.

'I'm not surprised,' he answered, 'when we got back last night, we found a wounded man and she had to hold the torch while I had a look at him. Not a pretty sight and very upsetting to the nerves.'

'Cordelia, darling, you didn't tell me, how awful for you. Was there a lot of blood?' She turned to her uncle. 'Is he dead?'

'Blood thirsty child. No, he's not. Who is coming to church this morning?'

Cordelia looked up eagerly but said nothing and he went on, 'The Schottenkirche—it's close by, we can walk there, the three of us.'

'I don't want...' began Eileen.

'No church, no Schonbrunn.'

'Fair enough,' agreed Cordelia, 'you can sit quietly if you get tired, Eileen. Besides it's one of the places we haven't been to yet and there's only a little time left now.' She had spoken briskly but inside her, she felt sadness welling up to choke her. She ignored it, to be sorry for herself wouldn't help at all; she would

go back with Eileen and stay with her until she was
no longer needed and then get another, similar job.
Beyond that she wasn't going to think.

That night, lying in bed wide awake and quite unable to sleep, she reviewed the day. Something to
remember and most of it delightful. Church, under the
guidance of the doctor had been interesting and lunch
together had been a decidedly chatty meal, with Eileen hogging the major share of the conversation, asking endless questions and showing an intelligence
which her uncle was quick to meet.

They got to Schonbrunn before two o'clock and
had gone at once to the Coach Museum, where they
had spent the greater part of the afternoon, goggling
over the earlier coaches, equipped, for the twenty-six
day trips to Paris, with what must have been the
equivalent of all mod cons, and admiring the tiny
coaches used by the young Habsburgs and the hunting
sleigh with its swivel chair, space for servants to ride
back and front and reindeer horns to support the guns.
But it was the Coronation coach which took up most
of their time, with its gold trimmings. 'Eight white
horses,' marvelled Cordelia, reading the descriptive
leaflet.

'I'd rather have Uncle Charles's car,' said Eileen.
They had ices before wandering past the long rows
of linden trees and into the formal gardens and here
presently, true to his promise, the doctor sat down
with his niece and Cordelia was free to climb leisurely
to the Gloriette where she stood and admired the
view, wishing that the doctor was there to share it
with her. Presently, she walked back again and since

none of them fancied visiting the zoo, and the afternoon was almost over, they had got back into the car and had tea at Sacher's Coffee House. It was crowded and the doctor seemed to be on terms with any number of people there. Cordelia was conscious of curious looks and when from time to time someone stopped at their table, she was introduced austerely as Miss Gibson. The doctor had good manners, but she had the feeling that he would much rather not have done so. She had acknowledged each introduction with a cool, correct, German greeting and made no effort to take part in the conversation. Probably he had felt ashamed of her, she thought miserably, she was so dreadfully mediocre, both as to face and dress. Eileen on the other hand, took pains to draw attention to herself, trying out her greatly improved German and laughing a lot. In five years time, mused Cordelia, the child will be a menace, with young men vying for her attention. Perhaps she should try and explain to the child that drawing attention to herself wasn't quite the thing…

They were on the point of leaving the café when the woman she had seen at the apartment paused at the table. Her greeting was effusive although she ignored both Eileen and her, something which the doctor had put right immediately. 'My niece, Eileen, and Miss Gibson, her governess.' He spoke in German and the woman replied in the same language.

'My dear Charles, still saddled with your two unwelcome visitors.' She gave a tinkling laugh and the doctor frowned.

'Miss Gibson speaks excellent German,' he said

drily, 'and Eileen has made great strides since she has been here. Perhaps you had better apologise, Maria.'

She said sharply, 'I'll do no such thing. A governess and a child...'

She made them sound like something the cat had brought in, thought Cordelia and caught Eileen's eye and winked.

'My guests,' the doctor reminded her and when she tossed her head and pouted, wished her a cold goodbye. She paused for a moment, looking at him, her lovely face full of temper, then she turned on her heel.

'Sorry about that,' said the doctor, 'I'll apologise for her...'

'Are we unwelcome visitors?' asked Eileen.

He lifted a finger for the bill. 'I admit that when you came I was quite convinced that you disrupt my ordered life. But I can promise you that you have done nothing of the kind, on the contrary you have grown on me—I shall miss you abominably.'

'Just me, or both of us, Uncle Charles?'

He had glanced at Cordelia, sitting, prim and upright across the table. 'Both of you. Will you miss me, Eileen?'

'Oh, yes, you're ever so much nicer than I thought you'd be, in fact I like you very much now. So does Cordelia.' She caught Cordelia's outraged look: 'Well, she hasn't actually said so, but if you ask her I'm sure she'll say so...'

'I think,' said the doctor smoothly, 'that I won't chance my luck—not at this moment. Now who's for home? I've got to look in on a patient before eight o'clock—I'll drop you off as I go to the hospital.'

'But it's only six o'clock,' complained Eileen.

'It will be half-past six by the time I'm there and I'm going out this evening.'

'Who with?'

'That will do, Eileen,' said Cordelia sharply, 'you're being rude. You've had a lovely day; don't let's spoil it with peevishness.'

Eileen had given an exaggerated sigh. 'Oh, darling Cordelia, you're being a governess again. I bet you wish it was you.'

Cordelia had shot a look at the doctor; he was sitting back in his chair, most annoyingly being amused.

'That's such a silly remark, I shan't answer it,' she said.

Eileen put an impertinent head on one side. 'You're quite pretty when you're cross, Cordelia.'

'Come along—you are keeping your uncle waiting.'

'I am a patient man, quite prepared to wait for what I want, Eileen, be good enough to apologise to Cordelia—you have been rather rude, you know.'

Eileen had smiled widely. 'I'm sorry, darling Cordelia, truly I am.' She turned enquiring eyes on to her uncle. 'Why is it rude to say true things, Uncle Charles?'

'It so often causes acute embarrassment to those who are listening,' he told her idly.

Cordelia, going over every word, wondered for the tenth time, just what he had meant. That he was embarrassed? Not likely at all, he must have meant herself and if he had it had been rather an unkind remark...

She had managed to keep out of his way for the rest of the evening, waiting until he had left the house before she went to the dining room for her supper, after seeing Eileen safely into bed with her own meal on a tray.

Cordelia settling herself on her pillows, thought that it had been a lovely day except for the last bit. There were four more days before Eileen's parents arrived, but she wasn't likely to see much of the doctor before then. And a good thing too, she reminded herself firmly. 'Out of sight, out of mind,' and all the rest of it. She was just dropping off when she remembered another proverb: Absence makes the heart grow fonder.

CHAPTER SEVEN

CORDELIA WOKE to the distant rumble of thunder and when she went to look out of the window it was to see the blue sky overhead rapidly disappearing beyond thick greenish clouds, tearing across the sky. She flinched at a great jagged streak of lightning and withdrew her head smartly as the thunder pealed again. It was barely six o'clock and the street below was quiet, so that the silence after the thunder was uncanny, broken almost at once by Eileen's voice.

Cordelia bundled on her dressing gown and went through the bathroom to Eileen's room, to find her sitting up in bed, looking awfully scared. She said at once, 'I hate thunderstorms, they frighten me...'

It hardly seemed the time to confess that she didn't like thunderstorms either, Cordelia arranged her features into what she hoped was a calm carefree expression. 'Nothing to worry about, love,' she declared airily, 'I doubt if it will come any nearer.'

The brilliant flash of lightning, followed immediately by thunder fit to burst her eardrums, belied her words. She jumped visibly and went to pull the curtains close and turn on the light. It went out almost at once and the next flash sent Eileen under the bedclothes with an earpiercing scream.

Cordelia advanced to the window and pulled the curtains back again, rather in the manner of one ex-

147

pecting to be bitten by them; since there was no light, it would be better to leave them drawn back, at least they would be able to see in the Stygian darkness. The next flash took her breath so that all she could do was utter soothing sounds as she got on to the bed beside the humped figure in it and flung a comforting arm round what she guessed might be Eileen's shoulders.

The flashes were coming thick and fast now and the thunder was continuous, the sky was dark and lowering and gave the room an eerie light, so that when the door slowly opened, Cordelia, was quite unprepared to suppress a scared squeak.

The doctor came in, put his torch down on the bed table and observed softly: 'Scared stiff? It won't last long.' He eyed the heap on the bed. 'That's Eileen, is it?' and as another brilliant flash lit up the room and Cordelia jumped. 'Why don't you join her?'

Cordelia, overjoyed to see him and nonetheless vexed at his facetious remark, found her voice. 'I'm not in the least nervous', she lied.

His low laugh was, she considered, positively offensive.

He came over to the bed and bent over his hidden niece. 'Come on out', he begged her, 'if you sit round the other way, you won't see the lightning and the thunder is only noise after all. Look at Cordelia, as cool as a cucumber.'

Cordelia cast him a speaking glance; if being a cucumber meant ice cold with fright, shivers up her spine and an icy feeling in her insides, then she was a cucumber. His grin did nothing to help, and since she was almost scared out of her wits, to burst into tears would have been a great relief. Beastly man, she fumed, loving him fiercely and at the same time disliking him intensely. The beastly man leaning across, took her hand and held it and it's comforting clasp suddenly made her fright quite unimportant. She saw then that he was fully dressed; not his usual elegant grey suit and spotless white shirt, but slacks and a thin sweater. She said: 'You're up early...' She looked at his face then; it was lined and grey with tiredness and he badly needed a shave. 'You haven't been to bed.'

He smiled. 'No—there was a bad road accident and the theatre's been going all night.' He wasn't going to talk about it; he gave his niece an affectionate tweak and said, 'How about all of us creeping to the kitchen and making a pot of tea; the storm is almost over.'

It was exactly what Eileen and Cordelia for that matter, needed to take their minds off the storm. The three of them went soft footed to the kitchen; the warmth and familiarity of which made Cordelia feel far more at ease, and while she made the tea, the others found biscuits and sugar and milk and with the blind securely pulled down against the lightning and the powerful lights on, they sat round the massive table while the doctor told them amusing titbits about the lighter side of his work until Cordelia realized that the thunder was rumbling itself away into the distance.

She collected cups tidily, sat the table to rights, and suggested that Eileen went back to her bed. 'It's seven o'clock. I'll ask Mrs Thompson to keep your breakfast until nine and I'll bring it up to you.' She paused on their way to the door and put an urgent hand on the doctor's arm.

'And you'll go to bed, Doctor. When do you have to be at the hospital?'

He answered her gravely although he looked as if he wanted to laugh. 'Theatre starts at ten o'clock I'm anaesthetising...'

She answered at once: 'Then you can sleep till nine o'clock. You must, you know, or you won't be able to cope.'

He didn't argue. He said meekly: 'Very well, Cordelia,' and she nodded her satisfaction; it was Eileen who darted a surprised look at him, but for once she had nothing to say, walking across the kitchen to stroke the kitchen cat, sleeping in a chair by the stove. It gave the doctor the opportunity to bend his head and kiss Cordelia on her surprised mouth.

As she settled back in bed, Cordelia reasoned with herself; the doctor had had no reason to kiss her; he could, of course, have been too tired to know what he was doing, it could have been a gesture of thanks because he was at last going to his bed. There was no point in brooding over it, she told herself with her usual common sense and went away to shower and dress. To go back to bed would be silly now, she could hear the Thompson's up and about and she would have to see Mrs Thompson about Eileen's breakfast and ask Thompson to call the doctor. She remembered then that he hadn't said anything about 'phoning the hospital; did they expect him before ten o'clock? Did he have ward rounds, she wondered, or consultations? Not only had she no idea of his private life, she knew nothing of his work. It was like living with a clam, she thought crossly, going off to discuss her problem with Thompson.

He set her mind at rest at once. The doctor, he informed her civilly, went to the hospital at eight o'clock on four mornings of the week, on the fifth—that very day, he had no need to go until ten o'clock. Indeed, said Thompson, the doctor could very well 'phone and say that someone else must go to the theatre that morning, seeing that he had been up for almost all of the night, but that wasn't the doctor's way. 'I've known him go without sleep for twenty four hours or more, miss—them bomb outrages it was, and the theatre at the London Royal going non-stop—nasty cases they were too, but as you may know, the giving of an anaesthetic is a skilled business, as skilled as the surgeon's.' He eyed her tired face. 'You go along to the sitting room, Miss and I'll bring you your breakfast; plenty of time for you to have yours before Miss Eileen wakes—so a nice strong cup of tea...'

She drank her tea and ate her breakfast while she thought about the doctor. She dearly wanted to know everything about him, but so far, all she knew were the few crumbs of information from Thompson. Charles Trescombe wasn't a man to talk about himself and anyway, he would hardly pour out his life's history to the governess. She collected the post from the hall table and slit the envelopes and arranged them neatly by his place at table. Then put the waste paper

basket on the exact spot where he was in the habit of
casting his discarded correspondence. By then it was
time to take a tray up to Eileen, whom she found
curled up like a dormouse, sound asleep. She set the
tray down, drew the curtains back and roused the
child. Eileen woke at once, thankfully in splendid
spirits; she had forgotten her fright of the storm although the excitement of it gave her plenty to talk
about while she ate her breakfast. 'Wasn't it fun?' she
declared. 'With Uncle Charles here and going to the
kitchen…' she giggled, 'I said he was fun, and he is,
isn't he?'

Cordelia murmured in a neutral kind of way; if she
agreed Eileen was quite capable of telling him that
she had and making her look a fool. She led the conversation away from him and enquired what Eileen
would like to do. 'There aren't many days left,' she
warned, 'I know we've been almost everywhere, but
is there something you want to see?'

'Shops', said Eileen, her mouth full. 'Cordelia, I
need another pair of sandals—the ones with laces,
they're all the fashion and I'm so out of date…'

'Have you any money?'

'Oh, yes, Uncle Charles gave me some yesterday.
We'll get the sandals and I'll buy you an ice.'

For a twelve-year-old, Eileen was very grown up.
Cordelia wondered, if she had a daughter, if she
would like her to be quite so adult about everything.
She thought not, although Eileen was a dear child.
But the question didn't arise; she wasn't likely to
have a daughter, nor for that matter a husband.

'Where's Uncle Charles?' asked Eileen.

Cordelia looked at her watch. 'Just about ready to leave for the hospital, I should think,' and heard the door of the apartment close behind him with relief. Probably he wouldn't be home for lunch and by the evening she would have regained her cool and be able to meet him in her usual calm fashion. She said: 'How about going to the shops directly after lunch? There won't be much time this morning and you can have another nap if you like and then get up.'

She picked up the tray and walked to the door. 'I'll be back in an hour or so.'

It was very quiet in the apartment; the Thompsons would be in the kitchen, she would take the tray there and ask Mrs Thompson not to go into Eileen's room for an hour or two. She was in the hall when the study door opened and the doctor came out.

She just managed not to drop the tray. The colour came and went in her face and she stood like an idiot until he took the tray from her and put it on the side table.

'And why do you look so surprised?' he asked mildly, 'I do live here, you know.'

'I heard the door—I thought you'd gone to the hospital. You'll be late.'

'Keeping out of my way Cordelia?' He wanted to know, and she disliked the silky voice very much. 'And although I make the habit of being punctual, I flatter myself that no one is going to say anything if I choose to turn up rather later than expected.'

'Oh, yes,—I mean, no, I'm sure you do exactly as you like. I didn't mean…' She saw his mocking smile and held her tongue. His voice was still silky. 'I won-

der what you do mean, Cordelia. I should dearly like
to know.'

'I don't mean anything,' she snapped, 'you surprised me...'

'That is at least a beginning,' he observed thoughtfully. 'Let us see if I can surprise you again.' He
paused on his way to the door, kissed her hard and
swiftly, and left the apartment, shutting the door behind him very quietly.

Cordelia stayed exactly where she was. He had surprised her, but he was full of surprises just lately. It
was a very good thing that she would be leaving Vienna in a day or so. She must take care not to see
more of him than she could help. They met at meals,
but Eileen was there then, and it was easy enough to
hold a casual conversation then, with the child bearing the bulk of the talk. Besides, he never spoke more
than half a dozen words at breakfast. She went back
to her room planning how best to keep out of his way.
When she got there, she went and sat at her dressing
table and studied her face. Very ordinary, she was
bound to admit, and certainly it didn't warrant being
kissed for no reason at all. She must keep out of his
way, she reiterated to her reflection and allow Eileen
to do all the talking at lunch.

There was no need; he didn't come home. They ate
quickly while Eileen changed her mind a dozen times
about what she wanted to buy. She still hadn't decided when they reached the Graben and they wandered in and out of shops until she finally found the
sandals she wanted, added a cotton top which took
her fancy and some exquisite and expensive hand-

kerchiefs for her mother, and then true to her promise, dragged Cordelia into Sacher's for an ice. It was well past tea time by the time they got home and Cordelia judged it prudent to ask Thompson if they might have a tray of tea in the sitting room so that she had a good excuse for sitting quietly for half an hour; Eileen, she judged was a little too excited and would be overtired if she didn't check her.

The tea came, and Eileen, impatient at the idea of sitting still, allowed herself to be coaxed to drink a cup and eat one of Mrs Thompson's fairy cakes and presently Cordelia cunningly led the talk round to clothes—a subject which always had the child's undivided attention, and an hour passed unnoticed. An hour brought to an end by Thompson's entry to clear away the tea things with the remark that the doctor was bringing home guests for dinner. 'And he particularly asked that you and Miss Eileen would join him and the lady and gentleman for dinner!'

'I shall wear my new sandals,' said Eileen at once and dragged Cordelia upstairs to decide what she should wear.

Lady and gentleman sounded a bit ominous. Austrian? she wondered and were they rather special? She persuaded Eileen to wear a silky top and matching skirt instead of the rainbow hued cat suit she had in mind and wondered what she would wear herself. There was really no choice; it would have to be the blue; she had washed out the blood stains and pressed it carefully and if the doctor didn't think she was smart enough for his dinner party, he would have to lump it. All the same she took great pains with her hair and face, and primed by Thompson, accompanied Eileen to the drawing room at seven o'clock exactly.

Uncle Charles was there, urbane in one of his grey suits and sitting with him was a man of his own age and a younger woman. The man was as tall as the doctor, fair haired with vivid blue eyes, and the girl was dark and beautiful; a big girl with great dark eyes. They both looked at Cordelia and Eileen as they went in, both smiling in such a friendly fashion that Cordelia smiled back.

'Ah, Cordelia, Eileen, come in.' The doctor sounded vaguely impatient. 'Eugenia, this is my niece and her governess—Gerard...'

They shook hands and then accepted drinks and Eugenia said: 'Come and sit here, Cordelia. I know all about you but I don't suppose Charles even mentioned me.' She didn't wait for Cordelia to answer. 'I'm English, so is Gerard; he is a surgeon and he and Charles were students together. Gerard's here to operate on some VIP and Charles will anaesthetise. That's tomorrow. I wondered if you'd take pity on me and show me round in the morning—I'm dying to go in one of those little carriages...'

'We'd love to, Eileen's parents are arriving in two days time and I'm hard put to it to keep her occupied without her getting too tired. We can take a leisurely ride round the inner city and if you want to go anywhere special, the fiacre will wait.'

'Super. We have to go back in the evening—Gerard's at St Clare's and he's got a list for the next day. We live in London—Cheyne Walk. Where do you live?'

'My stepmother has a house in a village near St Albans.'

Eugenia gave her a guileless look. 'Not too far from town in between jobs. Are you staying with Eileen when she goes back?'

Eileen, who had been sitting between the men on the sofa, heard that. 'Of course she is—Cordelia's going to stay with me for ever.'

Eugenia said easily: 'Is she now? I was just asking if you would both show me something of Vienna tomorrow morning. My German's fragmental so I hope you speak it?'

'Oh, I do', said Eileen proudly, 'I've been taking lessons, and Cordelia speaks it ever so well, doesn't she, Uncle Charles?'

Cordelia tried to look as though she wasn't there while they all looked at her. 'Well, I get by,' she mumbled and went pink and Gerard came to her rescue with a kindly: 'That's more than I can say for Eugenia, although she says *Bitte* very nicely.'

Everyone laughed and just then Thompson came in to say that dinner was ready.

Eugenia was quite beautiful, thought Cordelia, sitting opposite her, and her dress was gorgeous, no wonder her husband looked at her as though she were the sun and moon and stars rolled into one. She wondered how long they had been married; perhaps she could ask tomorrow; it would be fun having another girl to talk to; living in the doctor's apartment had hardly been a social whirl. Not that governesses expected that, but beyond one or two stiff conversations with Eileen's German teacher, she had spoken to very few people. Except the doctor, of course. She glanced at him across the table and found his eyes upon her and looked away quickly.

They had coffee in the drawing room and presently she caught Eileen's eye and accompanied that reluctant young lady to her room. She had thought to escape herself at the same time but the doctor got up to open the door for them and asked her in a voice which brooked no contradiction to return as soon as possible and keep Eugenia company. 'Gerard and I have one or two small problems to iron out, and I'm sure you two girls can find something to talk about.'

They found plenty; they had taken to each other on sight, and after a discussion, in depth, on the present fashions, they progressed to personal opinions about this and that and thence to a somewhat more intimate conversation, wherein Eugenia enlarged upon the delights of being married to a man like Gerard.

'How did you meet?' asked Cordelia.

'Well, at St Clare's. Gerard's Senior Consultant on the Chest Unit there and I was Women's Ward Sister…'

'How romantic. Did you fall in love at first sight?'

'Good Lord no. At least I didn't.' Eugenia dimpled engagingly. 'And Gerard isn't a man to show his feelings.' She added unexpectedly 'Nor is Charles, is he?'

Cordelia went pink. 'I don't know. How—could I? I hardly ever see him; I'm Eileen's governess.' She was silent for a moment. 'There was a very attractive girl here one evening…'

Eugenia laughed. 'I expect he's got half a dozen

up his sleeve—I bet he doesn't marry any of them. Gerard says he's a dark horse.'

'He works very hard.'

Something in Cordelia's voice made her companion give her a sharp glance. 'He's what they call an eminent physician, like Gerard's an eminent surgeon. They can't help themselves. Now, tell me, what shall we do tomorrow?'

They had their plans nicely laid when the men rejoined them and presently Gerard and Eugenia went back to their hotel. Cordelia, left in the drawing room while the doctor saw his guests down to the street, thought it prudent to go to her room and was in fact half way along the corridor when he called softly from the hall.

She had to stop. She turned round and asked: 'Yes, Dr Trescombe, you wanted me?'

'Indeed I do.' He held the drawing room door open for her and she went past him, to stand in the middle of the handsome carpet facing him.

'We'll have some coffee, shall we?' He asked and without waiting for her answer tugged the old fashioned brass bell handle by the ornate stove. 'You've arranged something for tomorrow morning with Eugenia?'

'Yes, thank you. Eileen's coming with us, unless you object?'

He sounded testy. 'Why should I object? I may not be an ideal uncle but I'm no ogre.'

She made haste to agree. And when the silence went on for too long: 'You wanted to see me, Dr Trescombe?'

'Sit down. My sister and her husband will be here in two days time. They would like to stay in Vienna for a few days—I take it that you are free to return with them when they wish. You have no other job to go to?'

He'd asked her that before; perhaps he had forgotten. 'No nothing.'

'Eileen would like you to stay with her.'

'Yes, she told me so.' She didn't add anything; Eileen was an indulged child, almost for certain if she said that she wanted Cordelia to stay, no one would stand in her way. She felt reasonably sure that the job was hers as long as she liked to have it.

The coffee came and she poured out for them both. 'I am leaving for London myself in ten days or so.' The doctor had gone to sit in his chair with the air of a man who had all the time in the world. 'Perhaps we shall meet there.'

'That's not very likely,' said Cordelia matter-of-factly. 'I mean, you're... Eugenia said you were an eminent physician—governesses don't mix with them.'

He said idly: 'But you will not remain a governess all your life, Cordelia.'

'I'm not trained for anything.'

He said quietly: 'You could live at home for a while and take some course or other. You live near London?'

She had no intention of telling him. 'Oh, I don't think I'd like to do that and I quite like being a governess, you know.'

'Indeed? You could conceivably find yourself with

four children to look after instead of one, all of them ten times worse than Eileen. Even a saint wouldn't like that.' He settled back in his chair. 'Why not train as a nurse? You have O levels, haven't you? A levels too probably,' and when she nodded. 'So there would be little difficulty in being accepted for training. I could put in a word for you at Clare's.'

She said too quickly: 'Oh, no—no, thank you. I don't think I'd like that.' And nor would she, meeting him, perhaps from time to time, and each meeting would rekindle her love, far better to make a clean break; go back to England and never see him again. She remembered then that of course he was Eileen's uncle and if she stayed as governess to the child, they would be bound to meet at some time or other. She would have to leave Eileen once they were back home—she wouldn't be missed when Eileen started going to school again—and get something well away from London…

'What are you plotting so busily?' asked the doctor.

'Me? plotting? Oh, nothing—just thinking.' She put down her cup and saucer. 'If you don't mind, I'll go to bed.'

She hardly expected him to answer this, nor did he. He got up and held the door for her. As she went past him he observed: 'Things have a way of working out, Cordelia—there's no need to fret your charming head too much.'

She gave him a startled look as she went and quite forgot to say good night…

She pondered that remark while she got ready for bed and came to the conclusion that he was referring

to her chances of staying with Eileen. It surprised her
a little that he should concern himself about that; he
had never shown much interest in her. And that's a
pity, she told herself getting into bed. She hopped out
again and went to look at herself in the dressing table
mirror. 'But what can you expect?' She asked her
reflection, there was nothing in her appearance to
catch the eye, especially the eye of someone like Eileen's Uncle Charles. She sighed and got back into
bed and presently she went to sleep.

She was her usual neat calm self at breakfast; Eileen, cautioned to contain her excitement at the idea
of spending the morning with Eugenia and herself,
sat through the meal in such a concentration of un-
spoken feeling that her uncle looked up presently to
remark, 'You appear about to explode, Eileen, if you
have something to say, do say it.'

'I mustn't—Cordelia told me to be quiet while
you're here, so that you are not disturbed.'

Cordelia watched his eyebrows lift. 'Surely a little
too stern, Cordelia? Am I so irascible?' His voice was
so cold that she blushed and then, peeved that he
should criticise her so unfairly: 'Yes, you are just that
at breakfast. We neither of us mind,' she explained,
'we know that you like to read your letters and not
talk and we do our best not to disturb you.'

'I stand corrected. Do tell, Eileen.'

'Eugenia's coming and we're going to ride all over
Vienna in a fiacre and go to the shops; Cordelia told
me just now—and she wants to buy things and I love
shopping. I think Cordelia ought to buy herself a
pretty dress too—we'll both be able to help her

choose it. You could take her out to dinner, Uncle, so that she could wear it.'

The doctor's gaze flickered over Cordelia's outraged face, he said heartily: 'What a splendid idea, Eileen. I'm glad that you're growing into a girl of sound common sense. Don't you agree, Cordelia?'

'I don't want a new dress,' said Cordelia, goaded.

'Now that is something I cannot accept—all females want new dresses. Besides, Eileen is so anxious for you to have one, and surely it is a very trivial wish to grant her,' he added outrageously: 'She has been very good and brave over her appendix and deserves a treat.'

Cordelia choked. 'A treat...I'm sure Eugenia's shopping will take up all our time.'

The doctor rose from the table. 'I see that you are determined to thwart the dear child and I will say no more. I shall not be home for lunch.'

He patted Eileen on the shoulder, gave Cordelia an intimidating look and went out of the room. He paused at the door and unobserved by the still fuming Cordelia, winked at his niece.

When he had gone, Eileen said thoughtfully: 'Uncle Charles has changed since we came here. Do you suppose it's us?'

'I really don't know and I'm not particularly interested. Eileen, it was rude of you to discuss me with your uncle, I'm annoyed.'

Eileen got up and wreathed her arms round Cordelia's neck. 'Darling Cordelia, I didn't mean to, really I didn't, only I do think it's a good idea for you to have a new dress. I mean, they are so pretty and not very expensive and you haven't bought anything for weeks. It isn't as though you're unemployed and you're coming back with us...'

Put like that it sounded sensible enough and almost for certain the doctor's 'what a splendid idea, Eileen' had referred to the buying of a new dress, not an invitation to dinner.

'Well,' said Cordelia slowly, 'if I buy one, what colour shall I get?'

The morning was a success for all three of them. Eugenia was borne off to the Hof Palace, settled in a fiacre, and driven from one famous building to the next while Cordelia and Eileen gave a running commentary; tiring work, so that they had to stop for coffee after an hour and since Eugenia had invited them to have lunch and there was still enough time, they drove on to give her a glimpse of the Schonbrunn Palace before going back to the inner city within the Ring for lunch, where they dismissed the fiacre and led Eugenia to Sacher's Coffee House.

'Gerard said most particularly that we were to come here,' she explained, 'and that you would tell me what to eat. Such a pity that we can't stay longer.'

Over a lunch of omelettes, followed by a Sacher Torte and coffee they decided to look for Eugenia's presents and then tackle the more serious business of a dress for Cordelia. Karntner Ring was their obvious goal, and here they spent the rest of the afternoon while Eugenia chose presents, and then, since they were hot and thirsty took them to Demel's cake shop, where they drank more coffee and ate enormous cream cakes.

Much refreshed, they began their search for something suitable for Cordelia. She had fixed a modest price, and neither Eugenia nor Eileen, who considered privately that there was nothing they would wish to be seen dead in for that amount, said a word, but began a systematic search through the bigger stores. Eileen might be only a twelve year old, but she had a very adult view of fashion, and she and Eugenia fell simultaneously on a shrimp pink crêpe dress, simply cut, and for that very reason, looking much more expensive than it was.

'Pink?' queried Cordelia, doubtfully. 'But would that be suitable? I mean I never go anywhere—I thought something beige…'

She was howled down and made to try the dress on. It was undoubtedly charming and suited her; although she couldn't think of an occasion when she might wear it, she bought it.

The afternoon was ending, shops were beginning to close and Eugenia said that she would have to go back to her hotel. 'Or Gerard will wonder where I am,' she explained, 'it's been quite super, and when we're all in London we must meet. Gerard will have 'phone numbers and know where to get you.' She kissed Eileen and then saluted Cordelia just as warmly on her cheek. 'I hope you'll wear that dress soon', she said, 'it does something for you.'

On their way back to the apartment Eileen said: 'Wear your new dress tonight, Cordelia.'

'No, dear. It's—it's for special occasions—you know, when something unexpected happens and you want something pretty to wear.'

And when they were back in the apartment she smoothed its prettiness and hung it away in the big clothes closet in her room. It had been a waste of money, perhaps she would never wear it; it wasn't at all the kind of dress she had meant to buy, but Eileen and Eugenia had been too much for her. Eugenia had been nice, she would have enjoyed being friends with her, but she was married to a successful man and they hardly shared the same background. Perhaps, thought Cordelia, swallowing a watery giggle, she would find herself being governess to Eugenia's children. Just for a moment the giggle was in danger of turning into a sob. 'Don't be silly,' said Cordelia loudly and went along to see what Eileen would like to do before dinner.

They were in the middle of a game of Scrabble when Thompson came along to see where they were and a moment later the doctor came in.

'Had a good day?' he wanted to know.

'Yes, thank you,' said Cordelia politely and left it to Eileen to give a blow by blow account of what they had done and where they had gone.

'And Cordelia's bought a dress,' finished Eileen, 'and it's very pretty—she looks quite different in it.'

'I hope not' murmured her uncle. 'I quite like her as she is.' He smiled as he spoke and Cordelia blushed and frowned fiercely when Eileen looked directly at her uncle.

'She says she'll never wear it.'

'Oh, yes she will,' said the doctor. 'This very evening. We're going out to dinner and I must insist that she puts it on.' He added firmly: 'And you will have your supper here, Eileen.'

And for once Eileen had nothing to say, nor, for that matter, had Cordelia. She sat with her mouth slightly open, getting redder and redder, her surprised eyes on the doctor. She said at last; 'Are you asking me to have dinner with you, Dr Trescombe?'

'If you would give me that pleasure, Cordelia. Half-past eight, shall we say?' And when she hesitated: 'We can iron out any problems about your departure, can we not?'

It was on the tip of her tongue to suggest that they might do that just as easily in his study but she remembered the pink dress; perhaps she would never wear it again, but it would have been worth every penny just to wear it this once and to know that he had approved of it.

She said quietly, 'Thank you, Dr Trescombe, I should like to come.'

He strolled to the door. 'Good. I've some work to do—you'll see Thompson about Eileen's supper, will you? I'll be in the hall...'

In order to steady her nerves, she played one more game of Scrabble before going in search of Mrs Thompson and coaxing Eileen to bath and get into a dressing gown with strict instructions to get into her bed by nine o'clock. And for once Eileen was remarkably nice and meek and obedient, so that Cordelia had more than enough time to get herself ready for the evening.

'Very nice,' said Eileen casting a critical eye over her governess, 'You're almost pretty, Cordelia.'

That from Eileen, Cordelia recognised as a compliment.

CHAPTER EIGHT

DR TRESCOMBE was waiting in the hall when Cordelia went to join him. She paused on the steps, surprised to see that he was wearing a dinner jacket. The pink dress, though pretty, hadn't been bought with an eye to grand occasions. She said doubtfully: 'Oh, I don't think I'm dressed...I didn't know...'

'The new dress?' he wanted to know. 'Charming, and just right for an evening out. Dinner, I thought, and perhaps dancing after that?' He smiled at her so kindly that her insides melted with her love. 'Oh, that sounds marvellous, if you're sure I'll do?'

He took her arm and opened the door. 'Oh, you'll do,' he assured her, 'don't you know that Vienna is a magic city and all women in it are beautiful?'

'Well', said Cordelia matter-of-factly, 'I must say I've never seen so many pretty girls as I've seen here, but they are Viennese.'

She got into the car beside him and tried not to get too excited. She mustn't read more into this outing than was intended; a kindly gesture at the end of her stay, a kind of thank you for carrying out his wishes to be left alone to get on with his normal life while she and Eileen were with him; without conceit, she considered that she had done that. He would be glad to be alone again, no doubt, with the faithful Thompson smoothing his path for him, and his work...

They were driving along the Ring towards the heart of the city and presently he turned into Karntner Strasse, stopped before a brightly lit restaurant, and observed, 'Here we are—this is typically Viennese and I think you will enjoy it.'

Would he enjoy it too, she wondered as she got out of the car and accompanied him through the plate glass doors to be met and swept into the restaurant by the head waiter. The place was almost full, the tide of chatter and laughter almost swamping the orchestra's playing. They had a table by the window and Cordelia, looking round her, thought what a delightful place it was with it's small tables and their rose shaded lamps, and the gilded ceiling and walls. And once she was seated the dress didn't seem so inadequate. She took a deep satisfied breath: 'This is wonderful, Eileen would have loved it.'

He stared at her. 'Eileen is an indulged child who has just about everything she wants; she's my niece and I'm fond of her, but she doesn't deserve all the delights she gets. You do, Cordelia.'

'Oh!' she was suddenly indignant. 'Don't pity me, Dr Trescombe.'

'Pity you? I think I envy you Cordelia, you have the capacity for making the most of what you've got.'

She bent over the menu she had just been handed, fighting the impulse to tell him about her stepmother and the dull thankless life she had led before she had answered Lady Trescombe's advertisement. She was saved from replying by his enquiry as to what she would like to eat.

When she hesitated he said easily: 'How about

smoked salmon to start with and then perhaps roast duck with black cherries?'

She agreed without fuss, only showing her surprise when he suggested champagne cocktails before they ate.

'But we're not celebrating,' she protested, and added ingeniously: 'I've never had one...'

'There's always a first time, and we are celebrating.'

'Of course—us going, you mean? We're very grateful for your kindness while we've been here.'

His faintly mocking smile disconcerted her. 'I seem to remember you saying something like that before. Would you like to dance?'

The dance floor was large and not too crowded and he was a good dancer. Cordelia, who had little opportunity to dance panicked for a moment and then finding that her steps suited his exactly, gave herself up to the unexpected pleasure of dancing with whom she considered to be the best looking man on the floor.

'You go to a good many dances when you are at home?' asked the doctor in her ear.

'Me—heavens no.' Too late she realised her mistake. 'Well now and then of course.'

'And now you are governessing you have less opportunity,' he suggested smoothly.

She agreed a little too quickly, so that he glanced down thoughtfully at the top of her neat head.

To her relief he didn't mention her home or in fact anything to do with her while they dined, and presently, after the duck, they danced again. By now, Cordelia, with two glasses of the champagne, the doctor had ordered, inside her, was past caring about the future or regretting her dreary past; the present was wholly satisfying.

Presently they sat down again and she ate a dessert which only a Viennese could have thought up; chocolate and whipped cream and fresh fruit and meringue, she enjoyed it with the pleasure of a happy child and the doctor watched her, so carefully that she didn't notice.

They danced again after that and then had coffee and since he assured her that it was far too early to go back to the apartment, they danced again. Much later she remembered to ask him the time.

'A little after one o'clock' he told her calmly.

'It can't be—' Her eyes flew to his face, blandly smiling. 'You have to be at the hospital in the morning, Thompson told me.' She went pink. 'I've kept you from your bed—I never thought...'

'I think I won't comment upon that, but I'll come to no harm through losing an hour or two's sleep. And what about you, Cordella?'

'Oh, I've had such a heavenly time. I didn't know...thank you very much, Dr Trescombe for giving me such a treat, I'll remember it always.' She looked round the crowded restaurant. 'What was it you said? The magic of Vienna—Eileen told me—you must love it.'

'I prefer England. I've a flat in London, of course, but home to me is a nice old house in Wiltshire.'

She wanted very much to ask him where it was, how large it was, what it was like but she was afraid

that if she did he would give her one of his horrible
cool looks and tell her, in the politest way possible,
of course, to mind her own business. She said instead
'Wiltshire is a lovely part of England. I don't know
London awfully well—I don't go there often.'

'But you used to?' his question was put so quietly
that she answered it without thinking.

'Oh, yes—with Father.' She stopped herself just in
time. It was imperative that she held her tongue and
when he went on gently, 'Tell me about him,' she
said hastily: 'Not now I think; I really should be going
back...'

'Had enough of my company, Cordelia?' The
mockery in his voice sent the colour rushing into her
cheeks.

'No, oh no, you know that's not true.' She didn't
want to look at him but fixed her eyes on his shirt
front. 'But please will you take me back.'

There was no mockery in his voice now. 'Of
course, my dear,' and when she looked at him at last
he was smiling in a comforting way so that she smiled
back.

They didn't speak as he drove back, only as they
entered the apartment she said again: 'Thank you for
a lovely evening.' She stood uncertainly: 'Good night,
Dr Trescombe.'

He came to stand very close to her. 'Do you know
my first name, Cordelia?' he asked.

'Oh, yes of course, Charles.'

'But of course you couldn't call me that, could
you?' His face was grave but he sounded amused.

'No I couldn't. It wouldn't do at all.'

He sighed. 'Life is never going to be the same again,' he observed, and when she gave him a puzzled look, he bent and kissed her swiftly. 'Good night, Cordelia.'

She puzzled again over that remark while she got ready for bed, was he referring to leaving Vienna? Or because he'd finished his book and found himself without the work in which he always was so engrossed? Or was he—heaven forfend—going to marry one of the beautiful women she had seen? Several people had greeted him in the restaurant, but not the lovely creature who had come to the apartment. She shed a few tears at the hopelessness of the whole thing and fell into a troubled sleep.

He wasn't at breakfast the next morning which was a good thing, for Eileen wanted a detailed account of the evening. 'Did Uncle Charles like your new dress,' she wanted to know, 'and did you dance and what did you eat?'

Cordelia described the food and the dancing and the various dresses she had noticed and forebore from mentioning Uncle Charles and before Eileen could think up any more questions reminded her that her parents would be arriving the next day.

'How about getting some flowers for their room?' she suggested, 'and you've a German lesson this morning, haven't you? the last. You ought to give a little present—we've time to walk across to that shop where they have those pretty boxes of chocolates.'

They bought a beribboned satin box, had it gaily wrapped and bore it back to the apartment, stopping on the way to buy roses for Eileen's mother. 'You can arrange them later on after Frau Keppel has gone. Remember to thank her, Eileen.'

She went and saw Eileen safely into the small sitting room with her teacher and went off to find Mrs Thompson. She had an hour free and there was surely something she could do to help. There was the guest room needed to be got ready and if Cordelia would be so kind as to make up the bed and put out the towels it would leave Mrs Thompson free to prepare the elaborate dessert she had planned for the following day's dinner.

Cordelia was glad to have something to do; she bustled round, tucking in sheets and shaking up the great duvet, disposing piles of towels in the bathroom and making sure that the clothes closet and drawers were lined with scented paper and that there was a book or two on the night table and notepaper on the small writing table under the window. The room looked nice although she didn't really like the rather heavy furniture. She wondered how the doctor's house was furnished and wandered out of the room and down to the hall, picturing what it might be like, so absorbed that when she walked into him on the last of the steps into the hall, she uttered a small shriek.

'Far away, Cordelia, what are you doing?'

She told him and added, 'Eileen's bought some roses, she is going to arrange them when her lesson is over. We bought a box of chocolates for Frau Keppel, she's been very kind...'

'Ah, yes. I must see her before she goes. Go and tell her, will you? And then come to the study.'

'Now what?' thought Cordelia, poking her head round the sitting room door with her message and then knocking at the study door.

The doctor began without preamble. 'Sit down. My sister 'phoned this morning; their plane gets in just after lunch tomorrow afternoon. I shall go to the airport, of course, and take Eileen with me. I expect they will want Eileen to themselves for a while so I suggest that you take the afternoon off; I expect you've presents to buy and so on. We shall have dinner here of course, you'll dine with us. I should imagine my sister will want to talk to you about her plans for Eileen but certainly not tomorrow.'

He wasn't the same man who had danced with her last night and told her that the pink dress was charming; here was the Uncle Charles she had first met, the man who had said that she was rather a dull girl with no looks to speak of; he was so obviously pleased that she was going away.

She said in a wooden voice. 'Very well, Dr Trescombe, I'll see that Eileen's ready for you tomorrow and I shall be glad of a free afternoon.'

'That's all Doctor?' She said as she got up.

'For the moment—there is a lot more to say, but that can come later.' He got up too and opened the door. 'In a few days you will be gone. It won't be the same without you.'

She made herself smile and said brightly: 'Well, no, it won't; you'll have peace and quiet and no worries any more.'

He smiled faintly and made no comment, only saying: 'And you Cordelia? You are happy to leave?'

She spoke very firmly, more to convince herself than him. 'Oh, yes, yes, indeed.'

She went past him and hurried to her room where she sat down disconsolately on her bed. She wanted quite desperately to have a good cry but there was no time for that; Eileen would be free from her lesson in another five minutes or so, and the child had sharp eyes. She went and washed her face and made it up carefully and brushed her hair smooth and presently went back to the hall just in time to wish Frau Keppel goodbye as she left the apartment. The doctor came out of his study as she was shutting the door on that lady and hardly glancing at her wanted to know if his niece would care to accompany him to the shops. 'A small present for your mother—but I have no idea at all, perhaps you could help me to choose.'

'Is Cordelia coming?' asked Eileen.

'I think we might give her half an hour to herself, don't you—put your skates on if you're coming, I have to be at the hospital before two o'clock.'

So Cordelia, left to herself, went back to her room, did her nails, went through her cupboards and drawers with a view to packing their contents very shortly and then, since the doctor's half an hour was in reality three times that length, she left the apartment and walked to the Rathaus Park and sat down on a seat in the shade. It was a very warm day, too warm to think seriously about anything. She gave up doing that presently and just stayed, staring in front of her; there was one day left before Eileen's parents came, and perhaps they would want to leave again at once despite what the doctor had said, and after that she would never see him again. A pretty girl might have stood a chance of at least hinting at meeting him again, a clever girl might have done even better. Being neither she had no idea how to bring this about. Presently the pleasant surroundings lulled her futile thoughts and she allowed herself to daydream. It was thus, sitting like a neat statue, her face rapt, that the doctor saw her as he drove along the Doctor Luegar Ring, listening with one ear to his niece's chatter and deep in his own thoughts. Eileen saw her at the same time and cried to him to stop and pick her up.

He shook his head. 'Cordelia doesn't have much time to herself, my dear, she must sometimes wish for an hour alone.'

'But she's my governess, and I like her to be with me all the time.' She gave him a faintly cunning look. 'Don't...don't you like her Uncle Charles?'

'She's what your Granny would call a thoroughly nice girl, Eileen, and yes, I like her very much. And if you so much as hint that to her, I shall wring your neck.'

'Oh, I won't tell,' said Eileen loftily, 'but it's a pity she doesn't know because then if ever she wanted another job, she could ask you for a reference.' She frowned. 'You would give her one, wouldn't you?'

'You may rely on me, Eileen. Here we are, I must go through my post before lunch. Take the present with you will you?'

'I'll put it in your study.'

He got out of the car and watched her go in the entrance; a nice child, even if spoilt, and much too bright. He strolled unhurriedly after her and went to his study and didn't come out until lunch time.

By then Cordelia was her usual calm self again, she replied cheerfully to Eileen's chatter, made various and quite unnecessary observations about the weather, replied suitably to the doctor when he suggested that they should take a drive through the city and take tea at one of the cafés, and ate almost no lunch. The doctor, with his eyes everywhere as usual, asked her sharply if she felt well and she told him in her sensible way that she found the warm day a little trying. The grunt he gave could have been of disbelief or there again, acquiescence.

She didn't see him again that day; she and Eileen went for their drive, had tea and since it was so warm, went to the park and strolled around, admiring the flowers and stopping for an ice. After dinner, Cordelia got Eileen to bed, for by now she was getting both excited and peevish.

Downstairs in the small sitting room, she sat down and did neat sums, trying to guess her future. She had saved carefully during the past few weeks, and there was every chance that she would stay with Eileen for a month or so yet, at least until she went to school in September. And if Eileen had her way; she would stay for years. But she couldn't count on that.

Presently she went to bed, still pondering her finances; she would have to have a new winter coat and a skirt and sweaters, everything she had was shabby and governesses, even if not encouraged to be in the forefront of fashion, were expected to wear clothes suitable to their surroundings. She slept finally, her last thoughts not of clothes but of Charles Trescombe.

The morning was entirely taken up with keeping Eileen reasonably calm, listening patiently to her endless queries about what she should wear. By lunch time Cordelia had her dressed, ready and fairly quiet and lunch, which she had been dreading in case Eileen threw a tantrum, went off well, possibly because the doctor exhibited no signs of excitement at the prospect of seeing his sister and brother-in-law again although he was ready enough to discuss their entertainment with his niece.

He was careful to include Cordelia in their talk, not, she felt sure, because she would be involved, but because his manners were too good to allow her to feel left out. But his careless nod as he left with Eileen was meant, she felt sure, to put her in her place, reinforced as it was by his cool: 'Don't forget that you are free until this evening, Cordelia.'

She said tartly: 'I hadn't forgotten. I'm looking forward to it.' A remark which called forth a slow smile which disturbed her very much.

Left on her own, she went to her room, got her handbag and let herself out of the apartment. She had hours in front of her; she decided to go window shopping and visit St Stephan's cathedral once more, and then treat herself to tea at Sacher's for the last time. She was aware that it was an extravagance that she could ill afford, but she might never come to Vienna again.

She went to the cathedral first, wandering around its magnificent vastness and then strolling to the Graben, where she studied the beautiful luxurious things in the shop windows and then made her way to Karntner Strasse close by. She was looking at a display of leather handbags when Julius Salfinger came to a halt beside her.

'Ah, the English governess. I have been hoping to meet you again. I did not like the things Dr Trescombe said to me, you know. You owe me something for that, Cordelia.' He had put a hand on her arm, and when she tried to free it, he merely tightened his hold.

'I owe you nothing, Dr Salfinger, and whatever Dr Trescombe had to say to you had nothing to do with me and was certainly not of my doing.'

'No? Then how was it that he was so well informed? I don't believe you; I think that you wished to gain his interest and that was an easy way. No, do not try to take your arm away, it is a small comfort to me to see you frightened.'

She said contemptuously, 'Scared? Of you? Don't be silly.' She put her hand over his and lifted his hand away.

And at that moment the doctor, driving his family through the shopping streets so that his sister might get a glimpse of them, slowed in the heavy traffic and saw them. His face went blank and his hands tightened on the wheel but only for a few moments; he drove on at once, pointing out anything of interest as they went.

As for Cordelia, happily unaware of having been seen, she handed Dr Salfinger back his hand, wished him a cold goodbye and walked away. She would have liked to have run, but that would let him see how scared she was. There were crowds on either side of the street, she lost herself thankfully among them and when she reached Sacher's Coffee Shop, she went inside and sat herself at a table where she could see the street and the door. But there was no sign of him; she drank her coffee and ate her chocolate cake, her pleasure in her afternoon quite gone, and then made her way back to the apartment. She had a couple of hours before she needed to present herself to her new employers and she could sit quietly in her room until it was time to change her dress.

There were voices and laughter coming from the drawing room as she went in and she walked softly down the hall, intent on getting to her room. She had gained the steps when the study door opened and the doctor put his head out. He looked, she considered, annoyed.

'Back early?' He asked nastily, 'was young Salfinger on duty this evening? Still, you had the afternoon together.'

She was so surprised that she could only stand and gape at him. What had come over him? Usually so cool and impersonal, even in his more friendly moments.

She said without thinking. 'Did you see us? We were in the Karntner Strasse. I thought the airport was in the other direction.'

'And so it is, unfortunately for your plans, I drove that way so that my sister could have a look round...' He looked so angry she expected him to grind his teeth at her.

'Plans—what plans?' As usual when she was with him, she became less than her usual sensible self. 'And we didn't have the afternoon together, what a silly thing to say…'

'Do not make excuses,' said the doctor coldly, and withdrew his head, leaving her as it were in the middle of a highly unsatisfactory conversation.

Made even more unsatisfactory by Eileen, who came bouncing into her room a few minutes later. 'I saw you,' she began at once, 'with Julius Salfinger. Why did you meet him? I thought you didn't like him; Uncle Charles said he wasn't your sort at all, and that I wasn't to play Cupid and you were to find your own love…'

Cordelia's bosom heaved with rage, humiliation and deep regret that she couldn't throw something heavy at Charles Trescombe's head. She said in an icy voice; 'Your uncle has no business to discuss me and my affairs and I am quite capable of looking after myself.'

Eileen flung her arms round her. 'Oh, darling Cordelia, now you're mad at me, aren't you? We weren't discussing you—Uncle Charles was giving me a telling off—he said you were a nice girl…'

Cordelia gave a hollow laugh. 'I suppose that is an improvement on being a dull girl with no looks.' She went on briskly: 'Now love, you'd better have a shower and get yourself ready for dinner. What shall you wear?'

A red herring which was a sure fire success.

Cordelia put on the pink dress; with temper and the unhappy nagging at the back of her mind, her face was pale and needed whatever help she could give it. She went downstairs presently with Eileen, outwardly composed, her insides frothing with uncertainty; Eileen's mother might be a dragon; a female Uncle Charles with cold eyes and cold voice; she could dislike her on sight...

Mrs Kinneard was none of these things, she was a youthful copy of her mother, with a sweet smile, a kind face, exquisitely made up and wearing a dress Cordelia instantly coveted. She came across the room to meet them and took Cordelia's hand. 'I'm going to call you Cordelia—you don't mind? Eileen has told us so much about you, I feel we've known each other for a lifetime.' She turned her head towards her husband, talking to the doctor; a thick set, fair haired man with a rugged, handsome face. 'Henry, come and meet Cordelia. You know that when mother wrote to say she'd engaged a governess we did wonder what she was like. Mother's no good at describing anyone, she wrote that you were just right for Eileen, Eileen told us that you were an angel who liked clothes—it was Charles who described you in detail.'

By a strong effort of will Cordelia didn't blush. She smiled nicely, darted a dagger look at the doctor who returned it with a bland stare, and patiently answered Mrs Kinneard's questions, sitting beside her on the sofa, sipping a very dry sherry which she didn't like much. The two men were at the other end of the room and Eileen divided her attention upon both parties.

No one said a word about future plans, it wasn't until Eileen had been coaxed to bed and Cordelia got up to go with her that Mrs Kinneard said, 'We'll have a nice talk tomorrow, Cordelia. Will you come to my room after breakfast?'

Cordelia, sitting by her window, enjoying the cool evening air, wondered what they would talk about.

Both men were at breakfast and for once the doctor hadn't got his handsome nose buried in his letters. Instead he said carelessly: 'Open these for me presently, will you, Cordelia? I'll have to read them before lunch.' He turned to his brother-in-law: 'Any plans for this morning, Henry?'

'Sal want's to go shopping, she also wants to see Schonbrunn, the Hof Palace, the Cathedral, and the Vienna Woods, oh, and Sacher's of course. How many days will that take?'

'It depends on the shopping. Don't rush away on my account—I'm here for another ten days at least.'

'I'd like to get back before the end of the week. I'll see if I can get Sal to agree to three days before we move on.' He smiled across the table at Cordelia. 'I hope you'll move with us,' he said kindly, 'My wife will talk about that. I'll take Eileen off your hands for an hour so that you can have your little chat.'

Which seemed a good moment to excuse herself from the breakfast table and go up to Mrs Kinneard's room. That lady was sitting up in the vast bed, a breakfast tray pushed to one side, leafing through a magazine.

'There you are,' she looked pleased to see Cordelia. 'Come and sit down and we'll have our little chat. Charles tells us that you've been splendid with Eileen, that she's been taking German lessons and embroi-

dery and playing tennis.' Mrs Kinneard seemed to
have forgotten that Cordelia had written faithfully
giving details of all these activities. 'I'm afraid she's
been spoilt but he assures me that you have dealt with
that most efficiently. She has become very fond of
you, which is nice, and I—we would be very happy
if you would return with us. My husband is anxious
to get home as soon as possible, but I'm hoping he'll
stay just a day or so so that I can have a look round.
I do need some new clothes—I dare say Eileen could
do with one or two things, I'll take her with me. What
time does Charles have lunch? If I get up now, would
we have time to shop before then?'

'Oh, yes Mrs Kinneard, you could walk—no, perhaps if you had a taxi to Karntner Strasse, the Graben
is close by, they are the two best shopping streets—
you could take a fiacre back here—the doctor has
lunch at one o'clock, but he is not always at home,
though I expect he will be now that you are here.'

Mrs Kinneard nibbled at a piece of cold toast.
'Does he still keep his nose buried in his work? Such
a waste. I'm glad he was here to look after Eileen
when she had her appendix. He's not as crusty as he
seems. I must say he's pretty good at being head of
the family.' She shot a quick look at Cordelia. 'And
you, you have a family my mother told us.'

'Oh, yes. My father died some years ago.' It
sounded in her ears like a reference and Mrs Kinneard
seemed to regard it as one. She murmured, 'Oh yes,
of course—I'm sorry and you are the eldest?'

'Yes, by ten years.'

Mrs Kinneard said vaguely, 'That must be a great help...'

Cordelia wasn't sure just what sort of a help it might be, but her companion, nice though she was, wasn't very interested. She asked 'Would you like me to tell your daughter that she is going out with you or would you like to see her here?'

'You tell her, will you? I'll never get dressed once she gets into the room, bless the child. I'll be half an hour, if you could get someone to get a taxi and see that Eileen's presentable...'

An hour later the apartment was quiet, Mrs Kinneard and Eileen had been seen on their way, Mr Kinneard had gone off somewhere to meet someone he knew and the doctor had gone long since to the hospital. The Thompsons were in the kitchen, Cordelia could hear the low murmur of voices as she stood in the hall deciding what to do. Mrs Kinneard hadn't said that she might go off on her own, on the other hand she had nothing to do. It was then that she remembered the letters she hadn't opened. She went along to the dining room and found them neatly piled on a side table and sat down to open them and lay them in orderly piles; bills, personal letters, any amount of printed pamphlets and a couple of catalogues. She gathered them up and put them on the desk in the study and went to pick up the waste paper basket and empty it. She was on the way to the kitchen with it when the doctor let himself into the hall.

She had quite forgotten his bad temper of the evening before and although he had said no more than good morning at breakfast she hadn't wondered at that. Eileen and her father had carried on a conversation in which he had joined from time to time, she beamed at him now and said, 'Oh hullo, Doctor, you're home early—everyone's just gone out.'

'But not you, Cordelia?' He sounded disinterested.

'Well, no, I'm not sure if Mrs Kinneard wanted me to stay here, in case they come back early or something.'

'Most unlikely if they've gone shopping, I'm sure she meant you to be free until this afternoon. Most conveniently so—Salfinger has the morning off. Use the 'phone if you wish...' He sounded as though he was talking to some stranger he hoped never to see again.

'I don't wish to use the 'phone Dr Trescombe, nor do I wish to meet anyone. I'm going for a walk.' She swept past him and out of the apartment and took herself down the street and began to walk smartly along the pavement. When she had gone a dozen yards or so she remembered that she had no purse with her, something which made her temper, already very frayed at the edges explode alarmingly.

She stayed in the park for an hour, dying of thirst and with nothing to do but fume about the doctor's strange behaviour. 'If only I didn't love him,' she muttered, 'if only I'd never met him...' The idea didn't bear thinking about. Presently she walked back and was grateful for Thompson's thoughtful: 'Ah, Miss Gibson, Mrs Thompson's got coffee ready, you look as though you could do with a cup. I'll bring it to the small sitting room, there's still an hour before lunch.'

The coffee revived her normal even temper, by the time Mrs Kinneard and Eileen returned she was her usual practical self, ready to listen to that lady's descriptions of the purchases she had made and Eileen's excited chatter while the doctor and Mr Kinneard turned a deaf ear and plunged into details of the return to England. Cordelia, sitting nearest them contrived to listen to what they were saying, hoping at the same time that the journey back might be postponed for a few days. She paled a little with disappointment when she heard the doctor saying that he would arrange to take them to the airport on the day after tomorrow. That meant one whole day left, she thought distractedly, not that it mattered if he was going to treat her with the icy ill temper she had had to put up with that morning.

'Pink silk,' enthused Mrs Kinneard, 'with the prettiest lace insertions, I thought it was cheap at the price—real silk and hand made.'

'It sounds gorgeous,' declared Cordelia, and wondered what it was, certainly not cheap by her standards if it was real silk and hand made.

'I bought two,' went on Mrs Kinneard, 'and found a long sleeved one for mother. I do like pretty undies, don't you Cordelia?'

Cordelia thinking of her Marks and Spencer underwear, agreed, not silk but pretty nonetheless. But it must be nice to wear pure silk...

They had lunch presently and Eileen was handed over to her care for the afternoon. 'Take yourselves out to tea,' advised Mrs Kinneard largely, 'we're going to the opera this evening and I simply must rest. Charles do you suppose Mrs Thompson could give them an extra special supper?' She added 'We shall be out to dinner shan't we?'

Eileen was inclined to sit and sulk because she wouldn't be going out that evening, but as Cordelia pointed out in her reasonable way if she was cheerful about it, she was much more likely to be included in further treats, so the pair of them played a desultory game of tennis until tea time instead of going out again and when the others had left the house, Eileen, who had behaved in an exemplary fashion until the very moment her mother went out of the door, indulged in a fit of temper which tried Cordelia's patience to its limit. It was ten o'clock before the child at last fell asleep and left her free to go to bed herself.

She would have to pack for them both in the morning, she thought tiredly and probably give Mrs Kinneard a hand as well. At least it would keep her out of the doctor's way, something she told herself vehemently she very much wished to do.

The day was very much as she had expected; Eileen and her parents had hired a car to take them out to Grinzing where they intended to have lunch and Cordelia did the packing, ate a meal off a tray since the doctor wasn't expected back until the evening, took herself for a quick walk afterwards and then settled down to the mundane tasks of writing labels, inspecting drawers and cupboards and checking to see that she had supplies of travel aids with her. They were to go on a mid-morning plane, she had been told and stay at a London hotel; 'our plans are a bit vague,' explained Mrs Kinneard, 'We'll have a little talk later on. We do depend on you, Cordelia.' She had smiled very kindly and Cordelia had felt a pleasant glow because she was needed.

There was going to be no opportunity of seeing the doctor before she went, that was pretty plain by now; he hadn't been at breakfast and although they would both be at dinner, they weren't likely to talk to each other. Actually, she did see him later that afternoon, she was carrying a pile of freshly ironed undies of Mrs Kinneard's from the kitchen to her bedroom ready to pack later on, when he came in. But he didn't stop; just for a moment he paused when he saw her but beyond a brief nod, he had nothing to say and walked past her to his study. Just for a moment she was tempted to go after him, but only for a moment for what could she say when she got there? That she was in love with him? Ask him why he was so angry with her? If he were going to miss her and if he wanted to see her again? Such impossible silly questions. What a lot of things one thought and never uttered, she mused, arranging things tidily on Mrs Kinneard's bed.

She was quite right, beyond the small attentions good manners demanded of him, Charles had barely spoken to her at dinner and when she had seen Eileen to bed Mrs Kinneard had begged her to pack the rest of her things. 'I'm quite useless at that kind of thing,' she explained, and 'I'm sure you're a dab hand at it.'

So she had folded clothes and packed them neatly

and then gone to her room because she was pretty sure that she wasn't expected downstairs again.

And in the morning she went down to breakfast to find that the doctor had been called to the hospital at an earlier hour. He came in just as she was leaving the table, gave her a cool good morning and applied himself to his breakfast.

The trip to the airport had been well organised; he drove his own car with his sister and niece, and Mr Kinneard followed behind in a hired car, with Cordelia and the luggage. Their goodbyes were brief; as he explained, he had to get back to the hospital, and they would be seeing each other again within a very short time. He didn't say that to Cordelia, of course, but shook her hand and wished her a pleasant journey. It wasn't until she was half way to England that she remembered that he hadn't even bothered to say goodbye. It was a good thing that Eileen kept her so busy on the flight demanding her attention, wanting this and the other thing, that she had no time to think of herself.

It was that evening, after an over-excited Eileen had at last gone to her bed and the three of them were sitting over dinner in Brown's Hotel, that Mrs Kinneard said cheerfully. 'Well, we've made our plans, Cordelia, and I'm sure you'll be glad to be free to go to your home.'

CHAPTER NINE

MRS KINNEARD'S words dropped like stones into Cordelia's surprised head. She sat very still, suddenly and sharply aware of her elegant surroundings, the well appointed table, the delicious food; they had all dulled the pain of parting from Charles, now they were a mockery, making Mrs Kinneard's remark even more shattering than it was. Had this all been discussed and arranged, she wondered, before she had left Vienna, and did Charles know? She drew a steadying breath. 'I'm a little surprised,' she said carefully. 'When would you like me to leave?'

'There, I knew you wouldn't mind,' declared Mrs Kinneard happily. 'Here's Henry saying I ought to give you a month's notice and I don't know what else, but Charles told me that you had a family and a home and you must be longing to see them and it again. It was coming over on the plane I had this splendid idea; we'll go to Scotland, to Henry's brother and his wife, straight away—Eileen will love it—she hasn't seen her cousins for ages, then we can come back and stay with Mother for a few days and get Eileen settled in a school. She's too old for a governess—you've been splendid, Cordelia, but I'm sure you'll agree with me...' She paused and then rattled on: 'We thought we'd go up on the night train tomorrow—there's no reason why we shouldn't go and see Mother, Henry—

just for an hour. You could hire a car. You don't need to come, Cordelia—perhaps you'd get Eileen's clothes sorted out—all those thin summer dresses— she'll only need a few of them—we could travel light and send the rest down to Mother's.' She paused again while her husband watched her with a tolerant eye and Cordelia sat like a block of stone. 'I have it; Cordelia will you stay tomorrow night here at the hotel and arrange for the luggage we don't need to go to Mother's? Henry will book the room for you for another night, won't you dear?'

She beamed at them both, sure that she was delighting Cordelia and at the same time getting her own way. Just like her daughter thought Cordelia, but I can't help liking her.

'And now you must be dying to get to bed,' went on Mrs Kinneard, 'we'll have breakfast at half-past eight, shall we Henry? You can arrange about getting a car in a minute or two.'

Cordelia said good night and went up to her room; a most comfortable one with it's own bathroom and every comfort she could have wished for. Hers for another night, and then what? Perhaps it would be as well not to think about that for the moment; she would have time to decide what was best to be done while she was on her own the next day. She lay in a hot bath until it cooled, her mind mercifully numb, and once in bed, fell asleep almost immediately.

Eileen, dancing in and out of her room the next morning, gave no sign of knowing her mother's plans and Cordelia forebore from mentioning them. In a way, she could see the sense of Mrs Kinneard's decision, Eileen would be going to school in the autumn, anyway, and a governess would be superfluous; to make the break now, when there was so much to distract her, was a good idea. And nothing was said at breakfast, only that they would be going to see her grandmother and staying there for lunch. 'And Cordelia says she'll stay and get our clothes sorted out; we don't want to take everything to Scotland with us, besides,' added Mrs Kinneard cunningly, 'There are some splendid shops in Edinburgh.'

So presently they drove away in the hired car and Cordelia went back to their rooms and started on the lengthy task of sorting out the right clothes for Eileen and re-packing them and then going along to Mrs Kinneard's room where she found the clothes that the lady needed to take with her piled on the bed ready to be packed in a suitcase, which meant unpacking two other cases in order to fit everything in. This done, she went downstairs to fetch labels from the desk and write Lady Trescombe's address on them and ask the best way to get them sent. By train, she was told, a taxi to Waterloo and then hand them in at the goods office there.

The receptionist was helpful and friendly. She said, 'You do know that your bill's been paid until after breakfast tomorrow? If you could leave your room by ten o'clock?' She smiled, 'the porter will get you a taxi if you need one for the luggage tomorrow.'

Cordelia was grateful. 'Thank you. I think perhaps I'll take it along this evening, that'll give me more time to get my own things packed in the morning.'

The girl agreed. 'If you go around half-past seven

there won't be much traffic—the dining room is open until half-past nine, you'll have plenty of time.'

Cordelia made a good lunch, realising that it would be foolish to give way to a weak wish to eat nothing when common sense urged her to take advantage of the excellent food offered; the future was uncertain for the moment; she had enough money to keep her going for a few weeks if she lived carefully, but living was expensive in London. She would have to find an employment agency the very next day—there would be a fee to pay for that too... She went back to her room and for once was thankful that the paucity of her wardrobe made packing a simple matter. Everything could go with her in her case and overnight bag. She counted her money once more, took forty pounds of it and put it in the zip pocket of the overnight bag, and put the rest into her purse. At least she wasn't destitute and she was prepared to take any job offered. To go back to her stepmother's was unthinkable and there was no one else. Charles' handsome unsmiling face blotted out her thoughts for a moment, but she brushed it firmly aside; there was no room for him in her life; Vienna had been a lovely dream and she had been lucky to have had it.

'You dare to cry,' she told herself fiercely and blew her ordinary little nose with an equal fierceness. She had herself nicely in hand by the time the Kinneards returned and a good thing too, for it was instantly obvious that Eileen had been told of her mother's plans and had taken exception to them. She hurled herself at Cordelia and flung her arms round her. 'You're not to go away,' she raged, 'Why must you

go home? Why can't you stay with me? It's weeks
before I'll have to go to school, you could go home
then…?'

'I've told you darling,' said her mother, 'Cordelia's
mother needs her at home, and she wants to go—it
would be very unkind of us to keep her. You're fond
of her, aren't you? That's all the more reason for trying to understand.' She added: 'She's not going far
away, you know; of course you'll see her again. We'll
find a lovely present in Edinburgh and send it, and
you can write… Now shall we have some tea? We
shall have dinner on the train, you'll enjoy that and
Uncle Roger will be waiting for us at Edinburgh…'

'I don't want to go,' declared Eileen, 'and I don't
want any tea…'

Cordelia kissed one tear stained cheek. 'I do,' she
said cheerfully, 'and while we are having it I want to
hear all about Scotland and your cousins there. You
must write to me, though I bet you'll have so many
things to do that you won't have the time…picnics,
and riding and making friends, and of course you'll
go shopping with your mother. There are some lovely
shops…'

'You've been to Edinburgh?' Eileen stopped howl-
ing to ask.

Cordelia remembered very clearly going down
Princes Street with her father stopping to look in
every window and having anything she fancied
bought for her. 'Oh, yes—I've visited it twice, a long
time ago, but I'm sure the shops are just as fine.'

Eileen cheered up a good deal after that, they sat
in the lounge having a leisurely tea and then it was

time to send for the luggage call a taxi and say goodbye. Eileen almost strangled her with her goodbye
hugs and Cordelia hugged her back; perhaps it was
as well that they weren't to see each other again, despite Mrs Kinneard's vague promises, Eileen was part
of Vienna, and best forgotten together with all her
other dreams. Mrs Kinneard kissed her too, delighted
that she had got her own way without Cordelia making a fuss—such a nice girl—she had told her husband, 'she'll get a job in no time at all, and she has
got her family...'

Mr Kinneard, who allowed his wife to do exactly
what she liked, agreed, shook Cordelia's hand, gave
her an envelope, and ushered his family into the taxi.
Cordelia didn't linger on the hotel steps; she had the
luggage to see to, besides the porter was looking at
her with a sympathetic eye—the same man who had
wanted to get her a taxi that day when she had come
for an interview with Lady Trescombe. She gave him
a quick smile and went upstairs. In her room she
opened the envelope. The week's salary she was due,
and another week besides. A cheque she would have
to cash in the morning. There were notes too; enough,
she supposed to get the luggage to the station and
despatched.

She put the cheque in her handbag, then she went
downstairs again, asked to have the Kinneard's luggage brought down and a taxi fetched and went off
to Waterloo Station. It took a little time to settle matters, but once done she got on a bus which would
take her near the hotel. Now she had only herself to
think of; perhaps the hotel would let her leave her

case there while she looked for a room and once she had that, she could go to an agency and take the first thing they offered. She sat deep in thought in the crowded bus, squashed between a stout woman and a weedy young man with long hair, there was a fourth person on the seat meant for three, but she hardly noticed that. In Oxford Street several people got off and even more got on but she was oblivious of the jostling. She got off, in company with half a dozen others, at the New Bond Street stop, almost swept back on to the bus by the impatient tide of people wanting to get on. It was when she reached the pavement and her fellow passengers ebbed away that she discovered that her handbag had been neatly slit open and was now empty.

It was a mistake to cry out quite loudly that she had been robbed; the few remaining people near her melted away with mutters of 'Hard luck,' or 'you'd better go to the police station.' Someone called out 'I shouldn't bother, Miss—it happens all the time.'

She began to walk towards Dover Street, debating whether it would be of any use to report the theft and decided that it wouldn't; the only thing which could identify her was the cheque made out in her name. She had no bank account so that anyone could forge her name; even her medical card and passport were in her overnight bag. And a good thing too. So that left her with forty pounds and thank heaven she had taken that out of her handbag… She reached the hotel, went to her room and changed her dress and went down to her dinner. She ate splendidly aware that she wasn't likely to get another meal like it for some time, and presently went to bed; so much had happened in the past few days that none of it seemed quite true.

She was up early and after breakfast arranged with the receptionist to leave her case at the hotel and fetch it later in the day. At the door the same porter was on duty. 'Call you a cab, Miss?' He asked cheerfully.

She shook her head. 'No, thank you, but I wonder if you could tell me whereabouts Wyngate Street is? It's off Oxford Street...'

She knew that because she had looked up the addresses of several agencies and somehow 'Mrs Sharp's Agency' sounded respectable...

'Other end of Oxford Street, Miss.' He added: 'Not much of a neighbourhood, were you looking for somewhere special?'

She told him and he nodded. 'There's a bus from the corner,' he advised her. She tipped him; even the modest tips she had handed out had made alarming inroads into the forty pounds. She cheered herself up with the thought that her excellent breakfast would keep her going until the evening; a cup of coffee would be enough at lunchtime, the thing was to get a job and find a room.

Wyngate Street was narrow and gloomy and airless but luckily the agency was at the end nearest Oxford Street. She climbed the narrow stairs following the sign on the grimey front door, and obedient to the card with 'Ring First', pressed the bell beside another, even dirtier door on the second landing. The room she entered was in need of a coat of paint and the services of a window cleaner, not to mention a scrubbing brush on the linoleumed floor. There were four or five women sitting round the walls and Cordelia, receiving no reply to her good morning, sat herself down. Half an hour passed before it was her turn and she opened another door to Mrs Sharp's office.

Mrs Sharp was stout, of uncertain age and boot faced. She looked prepared to snap off Cordelia's head and listened with a faint sneering smile to Cordelia's request for a job.

'Nothing on the books,' she said finally, 'you can't type and you can't do shorthand and you've no experience as a sales girl. The class of person to employ a governess or companion is away on holiday. Come back tomorrow, I might have something then. That'll be ten pounds.'

'What for?' Asked Cordelia, taken aback.

'Why for putting you on the books, of course. Most agencies want twenty pounds nowadays.'

Cordelia handed over the money. 'I'll come back in the morning Mrs Sharp. I need a job badly…'

'They all say that. It's you inexperienced educated young ladies who are so hard to please.'

'I assure you that I'm not difficult Mrs Sharp, is there anywhere near here where I could get a room? I have very little money.'

'A room? Well yes, there is Mrs Dyson, about ten minutes from here up the other end of the street. Third turning on the left, number six. She'll let you have a room but you have to feed yourself. Forty pounds a week. Come in tomorrow about eleven.'

She didn't raise her head from the form she was filling in as Cordelia wished her good morning.

The third turning on the left was slightly better than

Wyngate Street, the houses were red brick, flat faced
and without even a small strip of garden, but Cordelia
had hardly expected that. At least the curtains at number six's windows looked tolerably clean. She banged
the knocker and an old woman opened the door.

'Mrs Dyson? Mrs Sharp told me that you might
have a room for me, just while I wait for a job?'

'Come in dearie, yer lucky, the second floor back's
empty.' She began mounting the stairs slowly and
Cordelia followed, trying not to notice the smell of
cooking and cats and stale air. But the room, when
they reached it, was clean, furnished with an iron bed-
stead, a plastic covered table and chair, a chest of
drawers with a book in place of one castor, and a gas
ring. There were two shelves holding a saucepan, a
kettle and a large enamel jug and a worn rug by the
bed.

'Fifty pounds and look after yourself,' said Mrs
Dyson.

'Mrs Sharp told me that you charged forty pounds.'

The old woman shrugged. 'Oh, well, since yer's a
nice young lady, yer can 'ave it fer forty...money in
advance.'

She held out a hand and Cordelia took out the
money.

'No receipt, dearie, don't 'old with 'em, but I'm
honest and I can see yer are. There's a key to the
door, what about yer luggage?'

'I'll fetch it this afternoon. How does the gas ring
work? Fifty pence pieces?'

'Yus and don't expect me to 'ave change, ducks.
Yer'll find it quiet 'ere. There's six rooms all let.'

Walking back, Cordelia tried to cheer herself up; she had a roof over her head for a week, the prospect of a chance of a job, surely within a day or two, and roughly twenty-five pounds in her pocket. It would be cheaper, she decided, determinedly cheerful, to walk up to Oxford Street and have coffee and a roll each day and something like beans on toast in the evening; she would get tea and sugar and milk and a mug so that she could have tea in the mornings, and a packet of biscuits. She found a café as she turned into Oxford Street and had a cup of coffee telling herself that she wasn't hungry, and then she walked all the way to Brown's Hotel to fetch her case. The buses were fairly empty but she sat with her overnight bag on her knee and kept a sharp eye on her case in the luggage rack on the platform.

Wyngate Street seemed endless, she thought that she would never get to the third turning on the left. She went up the two flights of stairs, found the key in the lock of her room and went in. Her heart failed her for a moment, then she told herself briskly not to be silly, put the case on the bed, unpacked, opened the window as wide as she could, and went in search of a bathroom. It was on the floor below, with an old fashioned bath on iron feet, a cracked basin and a geyser which needed money before it produced hot water. She went back upstairs, examined the sheets with a critical eye, shook out the small, worn towel and arranged her odds and ends on top of the chest of drawers. That done, she locked the door and went back to Oxford Street and had a cup of tea and a bun and bought a few groceries. By now she was hungry,

breakfast seemed a long way off and her insides were
rumbling. She went into a fast food café and had another pot of tea and an egg on toast. She felt better
after that and walked back to her room, not noticing
her dingy surroundings now, deep in plans for the
future. Of Charles she refused to think, nor of Vienna
or Eileen; to cry over spilt milk wouldn't be of the
least use. She arranged her purchases on the shelves,
washed as best she could in the bathroom and went
to bed. Tomorrow was another day, she reminded herself, and she was only doing what thousands of other
young women were doing, besides, there would be a
job for her in the morning.

Only when she went to Mrs Sharp's in the morning,
it was to be told that there was nothing at all. 'Come
back tomorrow morning,' said Mrs Sharp, 'you can't
expect to get suited all at once.'

On the third morning, with still no job in sight,
Cordelia left the agency and went into Oxford Street;
there were agencies there too and she had seen a notice in a rather sleazy café offering work as a kitchen
help. It would tide her over until something better
turned up. It was mortifying to be turned down; the
café owner looked her up and down, said forthrightly
that she really wouldn't do, too classy by half. He
gave her a contemptuous look and told her to try the
Ritz. The agencies were a dead loss too; office work-
ers, high powered typists and telephonists, explained
the haughty young woman behind the desk, and the
second one wanted a fee of ten pounds before they
would even look in their books.

Cordelia had a reckless coffee and bun and went

to the British Museum where she sat for an hour, staring at exhibits from the Iron Age. The quiet vastness of the place soothed her, she walked through the streets until she could have her modest early supper and then went back to her room. Her morale needed a boost, she decided, and she braved the use of the aged geyser and had a tepid bath, the air was a bit gassy and there was a lot of steam, which considering that the water was barely warm, seemed strange, but she felt better after it, and got into bed, with an evening paper someone had left in the café. There were columns of jobs being advertised, but not one of them would do for someone of her limited talents. She turned out the light presently and lay in the pale summer dark and thought of Charles. A waste of time, she told herself angrily, he'll have forgotten me already.

He had done nothing of the kind; she had filled his mind and his heart from the moment he had watched her follow his sister through the gate at the airport. The memory of her slim straight back disappearing into the crowds of passengers was etched on his mind so sharply that he knew that he would never forget it. He had driven back to the hospital, where he had spent the rest of the day in theatre and doing ward rounds, to return to the apartment at the end of it to snap at Thompson and refuse Mrs Thompson's excellent dinner.

And the faithful Thompson, bearing away the uneaten food to the kitchen gave it as his opinion that the doctor was in love. 'Head over heels, if you ask me, Mabel, with that nice Miss Gibson.'

'And high time too,' endorsed his wife, 'and who could wish for a better wife for him.' She handed the coffee tray to her husband. 'Leaving next week, aren't we? Whose to say it won't be tomorrow or the next day?'

Thompson found the doctor in his study, sitting at his desk. Forewarned by his wife, he wasn't surprised when he was told that they would be leaving within forty-eight hours. 'Can we manage to leave early in the morning of the day after tomorrow? There are commitments at the hospital which I must undertake tomorrow, can I leave you and Mrs Thompson to see to everything? I'll take the car, so there will be no trouble with tickets and so forth. It's just under nine hundred miles to Boulogne—we'll spend the night on the way and leave at six o'clock in the morning. That should get us to London sometime during the evening of the following day...'

Thompson received the news with calm. 'We'll be going to the flat, Sir?'

'Yes, I can't make any plans for the moment, but we'll go down to Wiltshire as soon as I've found Miss Gibson.'

'Quite so! Sir.' Thompson couldn't quite hide the satisfaction in his voice. The doctor looked at him and smiled a little. 'I've several loose ends to tie up at the hospital, I'd like breakfast at seven o'clock if Mrs Thompson could see to that.'

Thompson was at the door when the doctor asked:

'How long have you and Mrs Thompson been with me, Thompson?'

'A matter of fifteen years or so, Sir.'

'Wish me luck, Thompson. I hope that you and Mrs Thompson will want to stay with us after we are married.'

'There's nothing we'd like better, Sir. Such a nice young lady...' He beamed his pleasure. 'I'm sure we wish you both the very best.'

It was a fine morning when they set off, the luggage in the boot, the Thompsons impressively calm and utterly exhausted in the back. Somehow they had done everything; dealt with tradesmen, the flat's owner, the various bills, the packing; they sank back in comfort, knowing that the doctor intended to drive steadily, possibly for hours on end and that they could doze at will.

He drove fast, going by way of Munich, Stuttgart and Strasburg, where they spent the night. It had been a gruelling trip although they had stopped for coffee and lunch, and mindful of Mrs Thompson's English tastes, tea, but the doctor didn't seem unduly tired, indeed, Thompson was of the opinion that if he had been on his own he would have driven on without stopping. As it was they were on their way again very early the next morning, much refreshed after an excellent dinner and a good night's rest in one of the city's best hotels. Thompson, sitting beside the doctor now, remarked that it would be nice to be home again. 'You'll be taking a bit of a holiday, no doubt Sir?' he enquired.

'Yes—I don't take up my appointment at the Royal

County for another month and I've this extra week—
I should have left Vienna a week today but luckily I
had finished my lectures and the last few days would
have been nothing but a round of farewell parties.'

He didn't speak again for a long time, concentrat-
ing on getting the best out of the powerful car.
Thompson, seeing his stern profile, suggested that
there was no need for them to stop for coffee, instead
it might be more convenient to have an early lunch,
something to which he agreed with as little delay as
possible before driving on towards the coast.

The evening was well advanced when the doctor
drew up in the quiet street of Regency houses a few
minutes walk from Wigmore Street. Thompson, that
most efficient of men, had telephoned from Vienna
before they had left that city; the resident porter was
expecting them, their luggage was taken from the car
and when the doctor unlocked his front door on the
first floor it was to find the lights on, the table in his
dining room laid, and the daily woman who came to
help Mrs Thompson waiting.

The beds were made up, a meal ready and the doctor's post arranged neatly in his study. He went there
at once with: 'I'll be ready in fifteen minutes, Thompson—don't stand on ceremony, you and Mrs Thompson must be tired.' He paused and went along to the
kitchen and thanked Mrs Bassett for having everything ready, poured himself a whisky and went back
again and shut the door behind him and lifted the
telephone receiver.

The receptionist at Brown's Hotel was polite but
quite certain that Mr and Mrs Kinneard and their

daughter had left the hotel on the evening following their arrival. 'And the young lady—Miss Gibson—with them?'

'Oh, she stayed until the next morning to send on some of the luggage.'

'She didn't go with them?'

'No, sir. I heard Mrs Kinneard saying something about how pleased she would be to go to her home instead of going with them to Scotland.'

The doctor thanked her calmly, sat for a moment in thought and then rang his mother. Bates answered the 'phone, expressed pleasure at hearing his voice and went to fetch her.

'Charles—where are you, dear? Home? How delightful. Are you coming to see me?'

'Not at once, my dear. Mother, why has Cordelia left? I understood that she was going with Sal to Scotland…'

'Yes, dear, but Sal said something about Cordelia being needed at home—she was a bit vague, I did wonder at the time if she had decided that she didn't need her and had made some kind of excuse. You see, I had the impression that Cordelia wasn't very happy at home…'

'Have you the address?'

If Lady Trescombe felt astonishment at the urgency in her usually cool son's voice, she didn't allow him to hear it. She produced the address and only then did she say, 'Bring her to see me when you find her, dear.'

'Of course,' she thought he might be smiling now. 'She's going to be your daughter-in-law.'

There was nothing more to do until the morning, he ate what was put before him and went to bed. Not that he slept; how could he with Cordelia's image imprinted on his eyelids?

He was driving through St Albans by half-past nine and by ten o'clock he had stopped before Mrs Gibson's door. In answer to his ring it was opened by an elderly woman in a white apron, looking harassed.

'Good morning,' he smiled from his tired handsome face and Cordelia's old friend the cook beamed suddenly. 'I've come to see Miss Cordelia Gibson.'

She cast a look over her shoulder and said almost in a whisper, 'She's not been here, sir...' And then as a door opened behind her, 'Come in, sir and I'll fetch Mrs Gibson.'

The doctor eyeing the woman coming towards him across the hall, disliked her at once. His mother had been right, Cordelia could never be happy with this hard faced creature, smiling too much at him.

He said with cold civility. 'Good morning, Mrs Gibson. I must apologise for calling so early. I had hoped to find Cordelia here.'

The smile became a sneer. 'I haven't the least idea where she is—she left home, the ungrateful girl, weeks ago. If she were to return I wouldn't let her into the house. She was always difficult you know, bossing her small step sisters and brothers. Gave herself airs, too.' She added without thinking, 'The governess I've got instead of her is much more satisfactory.' She saw the doctor's hard eyes and went on hastily, 'Not that she was their governess—just gave me a helping hand you know.' She switched on the smile again. 'You'll have coffee Mr…?'

He didn't say his name. 'I'm afraid I can't stay, I'm sorry to have troubled you.' His goodbye was courteous.

He had turned the car into the road from the drive when the woman who had opened the door stepped away from the side of the road. He stopped at once and opened the door. 'You have something to tell me?' he asked his voice warm and friendly and she didn't hesitate.

'Miss Cordelia wrote once' he was told, 'just to say that she had a job and was happy and I wasn't to worry about her. She said that as soon as she had saved some money I was to go to her. Worked for her Pa and Ma I did, held her when she was a little girl and fell over and needed a bit of comfort. She ain't had none of that since her poor Pa married again—and since he died she 'ad to work like a slave and look after the children—and a nastier bunch I've yet to find.' She paused for breath.

He said gently: 'I'll find her my dear, I'm going to marry her, and you shall come and live with us. I've a housekeeper who will certainly need help.'

She shook his hand. 'God bless you, sir, I'm that happy. I'd better go.'

He opened the door for her and watched her trot back up the drive and then he drove back to London. He hadn't learnt anything of Cordelia's whereabouts but he intended to before the day was out.

The porter at Brown's Hotel remembered him from previous visits with his mother. He fetched the receptionist who had spoken to him on the previous evening and went back to stand by the door. It was on his way out again that the doctor paused by him. 'I'm trying to find Miss Gibson, who was here a couple of nights ago. You don't happen to know where she went?'

The man shook his head. 'No, sir, but I can tell you this, she asked me the best way to get to Wyngate Street, she wanted an agency there—Mrs Sharp's. Not much of a neighbourhood as I told her. She came back for her case in the afternoon.'

He was left with a fiver in his hand, wondering why such a meagre piece of information had been worth so much.

Charles knew London well, he took the shortest route to Wyngate Street parked the Jaguar outside Mrs Sharp's Agency, and took the wooden stairs two at a time, rang the bell and went in to the waiting room, half full of women of various ages. He wished them a civil good morning, and since a young woman had just emerged from the door at the end of the room, went past her and walked in.

Mrs Sharp lifted her head from the book she was writing in and asked coldly: 'What can I do for you, sir?' In a voice which implied that she had no intention of being of the least help. Charles looking at her didn't like what he saw, but he smiled charmingly. 'A matter of urgency, otherwise I would never have come without an appointment...'

Mrs Sharp's features melted into a kind of smile. 'You say it's urgent, Mr...'

'Trescombe. And yes, it is urgent. I need the ad-

dress of Miss Cordelia Gibson—I believe she is registered with you—' He went on smoothly. 'I have
returned from abroad earlier than planned and have
been unable to let her know. We are to be married
very shortly and I don't want her to take another job.
She wasn't expecting me back.' A singularly truthful
man, he was quite enjoying himself. 'Her last employers referred me to you.'

Mrs Sharp hesitated. 'Well, it is my very strict rule
never to divulge the addresses of the young ladies
who come here—this is a very exclusive agency. But
since you are to be married...' She hesitated, 'You
live here?'

'I'm a doctor living in London,' he added the
names of the hospitals where he held honorary status,
'if you care to telephone them...'

Mrs Sharp, not easily impressed, was impressed
now. 'That is quite unnecessary,' she assured him.
'Miss Gibson will be glad to see you, I'm sure. There
has been nothing suitable for her. Governesses aren't
in great demand, although yesterday she asked that I
would put her name down for any domestic vacancy.'
She opened a box file on the desk. 'She has a room
at Mrs Dyson's. Third turning on the left, number
six.' She glanced at the clock, 'she comes in between
eleven and twelve o'clock, I daresay you will catch
her before she gets here.'

'I am indebted to you,' observed Charles and
smiled his charming smile again, and went back
through the waiting room and downstairs to the car.

Number six, even though it was slightly better than
its neighbours, nevertheless met with Charles' disap-

proval. He banged the knocker and when an old woman came to the door enquired if Miss Gibson lived there.

'Temporary like' acceded Mrs Dyson, 'second floor back, I don't object to gentleman callers but I don't want no rough house.'

The doctor fixed her with an outraged stare. He said coldly, 'There will be no rough house, madam, Miss Gibson will be leaving with me very shortly.'

He went past her and started up the stairs. On the second floor landing he paused then knocked on the door at the back of the landing.

Cordelia was standing at the window, leaning out, looking at the view of chimney pots without seeing one of them. She called come in without turning round, the woman across the landing had borrowed some tea from her earlier that morning and had promised faithfully to let her have it back before noon.

The door opened and shut, and since the silence seemed strange, Cordelia turned her head.

Charles was leaning against the door, he was breathing rather hard and she thought, erroneously, that he had run too fast up the stairs. He was also very pale and when she looked harder, desperately tired.

She put a hand on the window sill because her knees felt like jelly. She said breathlessly: 'How did you know that I was here?'

He didn't answer her at once but looked round the dreary room, neat and tidy because she was that kind of woman but nevertheless, dreary.

'Why did you leave Eileen?' He asked quietly and she answered just as quietly.

'Your sister didn't want me anymore—I wasn't really needed; I mean in Scotland there were cousins for Eileen and when they come back she'll go to school…'

He said harshly: 'Is that any reason why you are living in this hovel?'

'Well no—I had some money saved you know. Only my handbag was slashed and my money taken. I had a little in my overnight bag and I'm—I'm waiting for a job.'

She had kept her voice steady but at any moment she was going to burst into tears. 'I've got my name down at a very good agency…'

'I've just come from there. The old harpy who runs it wasn't too sure about giving me your address. I told her that we were going to be married.'

Cordelia choked. 'Now I'll never get a job,' she mumbled and sniffed back the first of the tears, then looked up sharply at the doctor's crack of laughter.

'This,' he told her 'is the most ridiculous conversation,' and left the door and swept her into his arms. 'Who cares a damn how I found you or why you're here—I've found you and I'm not letting you go again, my darling. I must have been mad to let you go.' He bent and kissed her slowly and with delight. It was impossible not to kiss him back.

'Then why did you?' asked Cordelia.

His arms tightened round her in a most satisfactory manner.

'Young Salfinger—I was jealous—I couldn't think

sensibly. And then when you had gone he told me that you had given him the snub of his young life...I knew then that I'd been a fool... I've been almost out of my mind hunting you down.' He kissed her again, in a masterful fashion which pleased her very much. 'Forgive me my dear love and marry me. I think I've been in love with you from the first moment I saw you; I didn't know it until the night Eileen went to hospital. Very sharp you were because I'd forgotten you were waiting. I wanted to pick you up and kiss you.' He smiled suddenly. 'You snapped my head off.' He loosened his hold so that he could see her face. 'Are you going to marry me, my dearest?'

'Yes, of course—yes, Charles.' She smiled in a watery fashion. 'I love you more than I can say.' She put her arms round his neck and kissed him gently. 'Later on you shall tell me how you found me— you're very tired, aren't you? Could we go somewhere quiet and you could sleep a little and then we could have a meal.' She added like a child. 'I'm hungry—I expect you are too.'

'My darling practical Miss Gibson, when did you eat last, by the way?'

'I had a poached egg on toast and a pot of tea yesterday evening. And a cup of tea this morning. And when did you sleep last, dear Charles?'

He grinned tiredly. 'I'm not sure. We'll go to my flat where I'm sure the Thompsons will take the greatest care of us. And tomorrow we'll go down to Wiltshire while I see about a Licence.' He let her go reluctantly.

'Toss your things into your bag, darling and we'll go.'

She opened a drawer and started to take out her scant wardrobe. 'I don't want to go to my home, Charles.'

'You need never go again, dear love. I was there this morning. Which reminds me, I met a nice elderly soul there who said she'd had a letter from you. I suggested that she might like to come to us...'

Cordelia, flinging things pell mell into her case turned to kiss him. 'Oh, Charles you dear.' A gesture which needed suitable reward. But presently she was ready and followed him down to the front door where Mrs Dyson joined them. The doctor's magnificent nose twitched at the malodorous air which met them from the open kitchen door, but he bade her a courteous if brisk farewell, and shoved Cordelia gently into the Jaguar.

'Where are we going?' asked Cordelia. She was by now in a lovely dreamy state, and if he had said Timbuctoo or the Tower of London she would have accepted it and happily.

'Home—our home, close to Wigmore Street, tomorrow we'll go to Wiltshire.' He gave her a quick smiling glance. 'I told you that already—you weren't listening.'

'Oh, I was; I just can't believe it.'

Presently he stopped the car again and she got out and she looked at the elegant row of houses. 'Here?' she asked doubtfully.

'Here.' Charles took her arm and went up the steps to the dignified door, past the porter and into the oasis of carpeted calm that was the entrance lobby. 'First floor,' he told her and started up the staircase.

'It's grand,' said Cordelia doubtfully. He stopped and put a great arm round her shoulders. 'You'll get used to it,' he assured her and kissed the top of her head. 'Nothing is too grand for you, darling.'

They went on up the stairs slowly, his arm still around her, to where Thompson stood at the open door. At the sight of them he let out a soundless sigh of pleasure; he and Mabel could look forward to a bit of bustle now; the doctor would come out of that shell of his and later on there would be children. The future looked decidedly promising.

But the two people on the stairs weren't bothered about the future; the present was all they needed.

Don't miss the reprisal of Silhouette Romance's popular miniseries

When King Michael of Edenbourg goes missing, *Royally Wed — The Stanbury Crown* **his devoted family and loyal subjects make it their mission to bring him home safely!**

Their search begins March 2001 and continues through June 2001.

On sale March 2001: **THE EXPECTANT PRINCESS** by bestselling author **Stella Bagwell** (SR #1504)

On sale April 2001: **THE BLACKSHEEP PRINCE'S BRIDE** by rising star **Martha Shields** (SR #1510)

On sale May 2001: **CODE NAME: PRINCE** by popular author **Valerie Parv** (SR #1516)

On sale June 2001: **AN OFFICER AND A PRINCESS** by award-winning author **Carla Cassidy** (SR #1522)

Available at your favorite retail outlet.

Silhouette®

Where love comes alive™

AWARD-WINNING AUTHOR

GAYLE WILSON

presents her latest
Harlequin Historical novel

ANNE'S PERFECT HUSBAND

Book II in her brand-new series

The Sinclair Brides

When a dashing naval officer searches for the
perfect husband for his beautiful young ward,
he soon discovers he needn't search any
further than his own heart!

Look for it in bookstores in March 2001!

Available at your favorite retail outlet.

Silhouette invites you to come back to Whitehorn, Montana...

MONTANA MAVERICKS

WED IN WHITEHORN—
12 BRAND-NEW stories that capture living and loving beneath the Big Sky where legends live on and love lasts forever!

M M

And the adventure continues...

February 2001—
Jennifer Mikels *Rich, Rugged...Ruthless* (#9)

March 2001—
Cheryl St.John *The Magnificent Seven* (#10)

April 2001—
Laurie Paige *Outlaw Marriage* (#11)

May 2001—
Linda Turner *Nighthawk's Child* (#12)

Available at your favorite retail outlet.

Silhouette®
Where love comes alive™

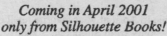

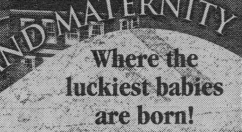

MAITLAND MATERNITY

Where the luckiest babies are born!

In March 2001, look for

BILLION DOLLAR BRIDE
by Muriel Jensen

Billionaire Austin Cahill doesn't believe in love or marriage—

he only wants to marry in order to produce an heir. Single mom and wedding planner Anna Maitland is horrified by his old-fashioned attitude. So when Austin proposes a marriage of convenience, will Anna be able to refuse him... now that she's fallen in love with him?

Each book tells a different story about the world-renowned Maitland Maternity Clinic— where romances are born, secrets are revealed... and bundles of joy are delivered.

HARLEQUIN®
Makes any time special ™

Silhouette®
Where love comes alive ™